$\mathcal{P}$AUL & $\mathcal{J}$ULIANA

Richard Hawley

ADVANCE READER'S COPY

bancroft press

Baltimore, MD

Published by Bancroft Press ("Books that Enlighten")
P.O. Box 65360, Baltimore, MD 21209
800-637-7377
410-764-1967 (fax)
bruceb@bancroftpress.com
www.bancroftpress.com

Cover and interior design by Tammy S. Grimes
Crescent Communications, www.tsgcrescent.com
Author photo by Jean Schnell

ISBN 1-890862-33-9
Library of Congress Control Number: 2003109115
Printed in the United States of America
First Edition

To

Kim & Greg

WHO KNOW THIS TERRITORY

CHAPTER ONE

"Can you see a young lady for college guidance?"

Betts Storey, secretary to the Guidance Department, liked Lawrence. She knew his responsibility was testing and measurement, not college guidance, but because two of the three college counselors were out of the office and the third was with a student, she decided to ask.

Lawrence considered declining. He was scoring and annotating a batch of vocational preference tests he had administered that morning. A boy, a junior, was scheduled to arrive in forty minutes to discuss the irregular results of his PSAT test. There was time to see the girl, although Lawrence always found it awkward talking about colleges or about adolescent futures. But why should the girl wait?

"Sure. Would you bring me her file? And tell her I'll see her in a minute."

Lawrence swiveled his chair toward the window. Outside, the lawn, strewn with curled elm leaves, fell away gently to the walkway and the street. The sky was glassy blue against the yellows and reds of the October trees. Afternoon light brightened the metallic finish of the parked cars and bicycles in the rack. There was no figure in the landscape. All was bright and still.

Betts Storey placed a manila folder on his desk. "Juliana Franck," she said, and left before Lawrence could swivel back to face her.

Lawrence looked at the blue identifying tape on the file's flap. He noted the ck ending of the surname, like the composer's. He opened the file and began to read the parents' names and occupations, and the names and ages of siblings. Lawrence suddenly felt irresistibly tired. He would have liked to lean back, shut his eyes, and sleep for an hour. He closed the file, looked again into the afternoon light, then told Betts Storey over the intercom to ask the girl to come in.

Lawrence did not like to talk to students from behind his desk. As he rose to take the upholstered two-seater at the front of the office, the door opened, and in this uncharacteristically expectant posture, he greeted Juliana Franck.

"Mr. Lawrence?" she said, her smile suggesting that something hilarious had just occurred, or perhaps was about to occur.

"I am he," said Lawrence, with a friendly, exaggerated formality.

He inclined slightly at the waist and shook her hand. Lawrence asked the girl to be seated on one of the upholstered chairs facing the two-seater. She thanked him but remained standing for a moment, preoccupied by the framed picture over the bookshelves.

"Sorry!" she said lightly, seating herself and smiling broadly again. "I'm Juliana Franck. That's a wonderful painting. What is it?"

Lawrence felt uneasy. The girl's beauty, so finished and so bright, had caught him by surprise. He cast an eye up to the framed print. She was right. The spindly-legged gothic youth and his maid formed a pleasing composition against the foliage of a stylized glade.

"It's called *The Swabian Lovers*, and it's by an unknown German artist of the 1400s. I got it in Cleveland of all places."

"It's perfect," said Juliana Franck, turning again to the picture. "Can't you just imagine them?"

"Mm," said Lawrence. "I think the picture's supposed to represent an idea. Probably 'courtly love.'"

"Oh," said Juliana, again the suggestion of humor in her widened eyes.

"What can I do for you?"

"Ah," the girl began with what seemed to Lawrence like a practiced relish. "I have a college problem. I want to study in the city—Columbia, if they accept me—but my parents think I'll be in danger there. They want me to go to a nice, safe, out-of-the-way college—one with a conservatory."

"Are you musical?"

"I play the cello."

Lawrence entertained an image of this striking girl playing the cello—her shining black hair, center-parted, falling slightly forward around her cheeks, her mouth pursed in concentration, her gothic form draped with a severe white blouse on top, a long black skirt below, knees bowed to accommodate her lacquered, burnished cello.

"Are you serious about it?" Lawrence asked.

Juliana brightened. "Yes! I suppose I am, but not serious enough for a conservatory or a career. Probably not good enough, either."

"Do you play with the school orchestra?"

"There isn't one, is there?"

"Well, actually—I should know that, shouldn't I?" Lawrence felt himself starting to laugh.

"I do play with the Ravinia Youth Orchestra—and with my family constantly. And I study with Nadia Godine. Do you know her? She's the first chair in the Chicago Symphony."

"No, I don't know her. So you're a serious musician."

"No, I like the cello, but it's just friendly. Maybe that's the problem—I'm not serious."

"Except about Columbia."

"Sort of serious about Columbia. New York seems wonderful, at least when I've been there—the beautiful end of the park where the Plaza and the big hotels are, by Tiffany's on Fifth Avenue—"

"That's not where Columbia is."

Does she remind me of somebody, Lawrence thought, *or is she all new?*

"No," she said. "Columbia's way up there. But I like that, too."

"But your parents don't."

"They don't seem to, for me."

"Mm. Where did they study?"

"Columbia!" Juliana said. "My father did. My mother went to Barnard and finished at Columbia. They went to school first in Austria, in Vienna, where their families lived."

"So you're first-generation native American," said Lawrence.

Juliana smiled. "That's me." Lawrence saw what it was about her smile. As the corners of her full mouth turned up, the corners of her eyes crinkled upward in lovely parallel angles. Involuntarily, Lawrence said to himself: *You're such a lady.*

"So how can I help you?" Lawrence asked.

"Ah—let's see," Juliana said. "Aren't *you* supposed to know that? My mother and father suggested I come in. I'm *in need of guidance*. Don't I sound in need of guidance to you?"

"I've seen more desperate cases."

"Oh, good!" said Juliana. "Do you think Columbia is all right?"

"It may be all right," began Lawrence.

"Oh, good! Then—"

"But, along with your parents, I might also recommend Oberlin, Lawrence University in Appleton, Wisconsin, and the University of Rochester. All three are actually more than all right, and they all have conservatories attached to them."

"Oh, dear," said Juliana. "I hope you won't tell my parents about them. They sound exactly like the kinds of places they've been discussing."

"For that matter," Lawrence continued, "if you're good enough to get into Columbia, you might have a look at Princeton, too. Princeton has a terrific music department, although you might find it a little far out, a little experimental. Princeton is also very pretty. You're probably less likely to be mauled or killed there than at Columbia."

"Do you really think Columbia is that bad? My mother and father do." Juliana seemed at least politely serious now.

"Maybe I've overstated it," Lawrence said. "But New York City is not like Evanston."

"It's probably like Chicago," Juliana said thoughtfully.

"That's good," Lawrence said, glad of the analogy. "I think Columbia is a lot like the University of Chicago, especially for undergraduates."

"Oh, dear," said Juliana distractedly. "This is not at all what I wanted to hear. Cruel, objective guidance." Juliana smiled wonderfully, then rose to go. "Thanks very much for seeing me without any notice, Mr. Lawrence. I'll bet you were busy. I may call on you again soon. I think I have to fortify my plan."

"It probably wouldn't hurt to give the issue some thought. You have plenty of time."

"Oh, that's good to hear. I keep feeling as if I don't have any. Goodbye, Mr. Lawrence, and thanks for the guidance."

"You're very welcome—oh, just one thing. I hope you're clear about what I did and did not recommend. I recommended looking around and thinking it over. I don't think Columbia is a bad university or a bad place for you to study. Do you understand that?"

"Yes, I do—and I'm glad. I may come back to bother you. Bye. Enjoy your picture." She gave Lawrence a smile, her warmest, in parting.

Lawrence seated himself at his desk and reopened Juliana's file. The inch-square photograph attached to the cover of the permanent record card captured the likeness, while exaggerating somewhat the angles of chin and cheekbones, the blackness of hair and eyes. The smile was true—open and warming—but with a crinkly suggestion of an understood, and perhaps shared, hilarity.

Lawrence turned the card over and noted, in addition to

her derived IQ (136) and PSATs (72 verbal, 61 math), the series of photos of her as a ninth-, tenth-, and eleventh-grader. She was there in each of them, he realized, but a little less beaky and less fawnlike with each successive year. Juliana Franck. The angles of her face, the light in her eyes, her crisp diction, appropriate wit, the ease of her laughter, the very music of her name—it all cohered.

Lawrence turned the record card over to the front. Her uniformly good grades, recorded by quarter, semester, and year, seemed to dull his impression of her. His gaze rose to the personal data typed in at the top of the card. Columbia and Barnard were listed under Parents' Education. Her mother's occupation was recorded as Housewife/Restaurant Reviewer. Her father's was shown as Executive, Hart Schaffner and Marx. Three sisters were named, all younger. Lawrence noted the address: a quiet, well-settled street a block or two from the university stadium, a street he frequently walked after dark. He felt unexplainably happy to know she lived so close.

"The Berrisford boy stopped by," said Betts Storey over the intercom. "He went to his locker and said he'll be back in five minutes."

"Okay. Will you bring me his file before he comes?"

Beyond the window, two brightly dressed girls, clutching books to their chests, ambled slowly along the leaf-covered walk. Lawrence's thoughts returned to Juliana Franck.

Betts Storey entered, extracted Juliana's file from the out-tray, and placed another manila file in the center of his blotter. "Berrisford, Paul," she said.

"Thanks, Betts. Could you hold him off for a bit while I look this over?"

Lawrence could not quite recall why he had made this appointment. Inside the file, clipped to the permanent record card, was a penciled note in his own hand. "Sections not completed, 10th grade PSAT. See before Jr. PSAT date."

He remembered now. He flipped over the card and noted the sophomore PSAT scores: verbal 52, math 20. The derived IQ scores from middle school and high school were 145 and 152. 152! An individually administered Wechsler IQ battery had been given the boy the past spring, Lawrence noted. There were no photographs on the card. Rummaging back into the file, Lawrence saw a small school photo appended to the boy's middle school transcript. It showed a cute boy-pretty face under a messy tousle of hair. The boy's teeth had come in strikingly large.

Lawrence was suddenly aware that he had lost track of time. The boy, Paul Berrisford, would be waiting outside. Lawrence thumbed quickly to the last sheet in the folder—a duplicate PSAT answer form he had received from the College Board at Princeton. He looked dully at the grid with its nonsense patterns of darkened-in circles.

Then he saw what he was looking for. The columns given over to the mathematics questions had been untouched. Lawrence looked once more, closely, at the photo of the disheveled seventh-grader.

"Would you send Paul Berrisford in, please?" he asked over the intercom.

Lawrence rose and opened the office door.

"Paul Berrisford?"

"Hi."

Lawrence shook hands with a rangy youth. His hair, though trimmed neatly around the ears and neck, was wildly unkempt, its matted brown-and-blond streaks falling haphazardly on either side of the faintest suggestion of a part. Ruddy, trim, and smooth-cheeked, the boy glowed with health. His large-mouthed smile—formed by prominent, good teeth—indicated some apprehension.

"Why not sit down over here?" Lawrence motioned to the two-seater.

"Okay."

"Have you any idea why I asked to see you?"

"No, not really—something about college?"

"No. Not yet. It's about the PSATs coming up. Do you remember taking the practice test last year?"

Paul Berrisford widened his eyes in exaggerated reflection. "Um—practice test? Right! I'm sure I took it, but I can't really remember."

"Yes, you did take the test. It's normally a junior-year test, but we give it to the sophomores as a practice test. It gives you a chance to see what a PSAT is like, and it sometimes tells us something about strengths and weaknesses." Lawrence paused. "You don't remember it? It takes the better part of a morning."

"No, I'm sorry, I don't."

Lawrence noted that, in a distinctively careless way, the boy was well dressed. Worn, clean, buff-colored corduroy trousers fell over a pair of ankle-length hunting boots. He wore a new-looking herringbone jacket over an equally striking flannel shirt, the collar tabs of which stuck out rakishly from the heavy cloth of the jacket's lapels. It occurred to Lawrence that not since Yale had he seen a youth wearing a sports jacket for casual attire. So far as Lawrence was aware, that particular prep school convention had never enjoyed a vogue at the high school.

"The reason I wanted to see you is that your performance on last year's PSAT was irregular. You don't seem to have done any of the math questions."

"Okay—now I remember that test. The long one with the math and verbal parts—the College Board?"

"That's the one," said Lawrence. "And you seem to have done none of the math questions."

"Yes. I remember that. That was a terrible morning."

"Were you ill?"

"No, not ill." Paul Berrisford shifted his position on the two-seater. There was, Lawrence decided, something leonine about this boy. Like an edgy thoroughbred, he seemed uncomfortable in the confinement of a school office. Perhaps he *was* uncomfortable in the confinement of school. Yes. Even his clothes seemed to be only tentatively related to torso, wrist, and shin.

"When I was taking that test," Paul continued, "I remember feeling like I wanted to scream. The—"

"Just on the mathematics section?" asked Lawrence.

"No. I didn't even think about the mathematics part. I had quit by that part. It was the other sections. The paragraphs. Do you know? There are those short paragraphs describing some topic—maybe about the life cycle of butterflies or somebody taking a walk. Then there are about fifteen very nit-picky questions about little points in the paragraph. It felt like being cross-examined about nothing. It was as if they were trying to be intentionally boring. It felt like they were teasing you."

"The test questions aren't always interesting." Lawrence remembered seeing the short essay on butterflies.

"It was probably stupid," Paul said, "but after about forty-five minutes of that test, I started filling in the answers without looking at the questions. I just couldn't stand that squeezed feeling anymore."

"Did you feel especially squeezed about math?"

"No. I don't mind math. In fact, I think I'm fairly good at math. No, by the time I got to the math section, I just stopped. I was feeling terrible. I just put my head down on the table and stopped."

"Do you think you'll feel differently when you take the actual PSAT? Your group is taking it a week from tomorrow."

"I don't know."

"One thing you might think about," said Lawrence, "is that the PSAT can do you some good if you do well on it. The National Merit Scholarships are based on the pre-SAT score, and being a finalist can give you a boost getting into college."

Paul Berrisford looked away, toward the window.

"Have you thought at all about college?" Lawrence asked.

"No, I haven't."

"The reason I ask is that, as you may know by now, your tested aptitude is very high. If and when you decide to get serious about school work, you'll have excellent college prospects."

"Umm."

Lawrence felt the boy disengaging himself from the interview.

"Where did your parents study?" Lawrence was aware, unpleasantly, that he had asked the same question with precisely the same words to Juliana Franck an hour earlier.

"My parents? Everywhere. My father is from San Francisco, and he went to Stanford, then to Oxford in England, then to the Chicago Art Institute for some special degree in film. He makes TV commercials."

Paul revealed this information as if it were not quite agreeable to do so, as if it had been, perhaps painfully, requested of him many times before. "And my mother went to Smith College, then to the Sorbonne in France, then also to the Art Institute. She illustrates children's books. My three sisters are in college now. Two go to Williams and one just started at Reed in Portland, Oregon."

"That sounds, among other things, awfully expensive."

"I guess it is."

"And what about you, Paul? Haven't you any college plans?"

"Uh, no, I don't, I'm afraid."

Lawrence wished he had looked more systematically through Paul Berrisford's file. He felt tied up, unhelpful—that he was irritating the boy.

"Are you concerned at all about the squeezed feeling you told me you had during the test?"

"No, I'm okay, I think. It's just the tests."

"It sounds to me as if you might be fighting them."

"Fighting them?" Paul paused to consider. "No, I don't

think so. I mean, I don't like them, but it's nothing big. Being in a room like that all morning, reading those paragraphs and those comparison tricks—'door is to knob as pitcher is to spout,' you know—it just feels like somebody is fooling around with you. Does that make sense to you?"

Lawrence was touched by the sincerity of the boy's question.

"I think it does. Tell me more."

"I may actually know what it is. The tests—and this happens sometimes in regular classes—treat you as if you're automatically going to care about them and try hard. As you said before, they're the big credential for college, which you're also supposed to care about automatically. But maybe you don't."

"And *you* don't?"

"You know, I really don't. Maybe something will change, but I just don't. A lot of them, the colleges, are really nice-looking places—I've seen Oxford and Stanford and Williams, and I've been around Northwestern all my life. But it just seems like a lot more time doing set-up exercises. More time standing around."

"You don't think there are important things to learn in colleges?"

"I'm sure there are things to learn. It's just that—and this may only be true for me—I feel I'm going to learn what I need anyway. I've actually had the feeling—ask my parents, we've had this out about ten thousand times—that school stops me from learning. School—Chemistry or American Government or the Film as Literature course—makes you *pretend* to learn. I mean, why not watch the greatest movies you can, over and over? Why not work with a crew on a film, then make one yourself? Why all the pretending?"

Lawrence started to answer but quickly caught himself. Increasingly, he found himself entrapped in an agreement with the adolescents assigned to him for counseling. *Do I feel this way more when I'm tired?*

"Excuse me, but what time is it?" Paul asked, lurching forward.

"It's twenty minutes to four."

"Oh, my god," said Paul. "I've blown it. I've got to run."

"Yes, we've gone past school hours, haven't we?"

Paul rose up on his toes, stretching. "I'm supposed to be playing the guitar, starting ten minutes ago, at the Northwestern Student Union."

"I'm sorry. Can I find you a ride?"

"No, thanks, that's nice of you. I've got a bike."

"Well, good luck. I'm glad to have met you, Paul."

"You, too. Thanks."

"Why don't we talk again? I'd like to hear more about how you see school."

"Sure," said Paul, his hand on the knob of the open door.

Lawrence noted again the high color in the boy's cheeks, the almost animal sense of being about to spring. "I'd like that. I could certainly use it."

They shook hands, and Paul Berrisford left the office.

CHAPTER *Two*

For Lawrence, Paul and Juliana's story had begun the day of that initial meeting. He was deeply interested in both of them. His thoughts hastened to them, separately and together, the instant practical business ceased to claim his attention, especially during the protracted hours between retiring and sleep, and between waking and rising. By his second or third meeting with them, Paul and Juliana had come to be brighter, more vividly colored selves than anyone else in his experience—including himself. Without being self-centered, they seemed to be instinctively aware of their personal importance.

Each of them seemed driven: Paul's latent animalism only barely meeting the conventions of modern suburban boyhood; Juliana, by contrast, too finely cultured to be contained by Evanston's prevailing conventions for teenaged girls. To Lawrence, there seemed a distinct unreality—or a surpassing reality—about them both. Their engagement in school courses, in the society of the high school, and in their music outside of school, was not quite complete. Yet it was not openly antagonistic, either.

Lawrence first became aware of Paul's unrelatedness to

school life when he stopped to watch a varsity soccer game on his way home from school one raw, overcast afternoon, late in the season. Lawrence, by no means a fan, had purposely arranged to be there. Paul's file had indicated that he played varsity soccer, and Lawrence wanted to know what he looked like in that context.

As Lawrence moved over the soggy turf to the sideline, he spotted Paul almost at once, standing a few feet from the team bench, his arms folded across his chest. Lawrence could see that his legs were mud-spattered, and his honey-and-straw hair was wet with rain or exertion, or both. He moved in place to the action on the field, but unlike the players on the bench, he did not shout or cheer.

The players on the muddy field swept in tortured clusters back and forth through Lawrence's preoccupied field of vision. The cold, wet grayness of late afternoon seemed to mute even the hoarse instructions and desperate appeals of the players.

"Berrisford," shouted the coach from the midfield sideline. "Go back in for Parini at right full."

Paul loped out onto the darkening field, slapping the hand of the boy he replaced. To Lawrence, Paul looked glad of the opportunity for release, for action. He played with a pleasing combination of passion, precision, courage, and, so far as Lawrence could tell, effectiveness. When challenging opponents for possession of the ball, or controlling the ball before passing, Paul displayed a delicate, even balletic, skill.

Yet Paul seemed somehow to lack involvement in the competition. After a pass or a long kick downfield, he sometimes hesitated before following the action on foot. His commitment seemed to be to the move itself, rather than its part in the desperate, erratic process of advancing the ball downfield toward the goal.

Lawrence paused in speculation as he watched Paul challenge an opponent. His sliding tackle over the muck of worn, wet turf was graceful and sure. But—again Lawrence saw it—the dramatic completion of the slide seemed to command Paul's full attention. In fact, the tackle, from his initial leaning backward until he resumed his standing position, was performed almost as if it were a demonstration of the Slide Tackle executed for instructional purposes. Paul's play, Lawrence decided, consisted of these nicely turned moves, privately executed and privately enjoyed. His kicks and tackles and passes might almost have been the solitary execution of a more highly ritualistic sport, such as karate or judo.

Shortly after darkness had begun to obscure most of the play from view, the game ended, apparently a scoreless tie. Lawrence headed home to his carriage house, glad no longer to be standing in the evening chill.

The next morning, early, during his break period, Lawrence spotted Jerry Stein, the instrumental-music teacher, at the coffee urn.

"Jerry," Lawrence said, "have you got a minute?"

"Sure. What's up?"

"I wondered if you could tell me something about a student who I think might have some talent in music."

"Sure. Who?"

"A senior. Her name is Juliana Franck. She plays the cello."

"The cello. You know we don't use cellos in the stage band. Tim Reimer has a few string students, but they're mostly beginners. I don't think he's got any Juliana Franck . . . *Juliana Franck.* Tell me what she looks like. Is she a dark-haired girl?"

"Yes, she is. Dark hair, sort of slender, attractive—"

"I think I know . . . Yes, I know Juliana Franck. Hilton had her in freshman and sophomore chorus and turned cartwheels to get her into small ensemble, but she stopped singing after her sophomore year. She said she couldn't fit it in anymore. Hilton said she had a wonderful alto voice and could read anything. Then out of the blue she came up to him last spring and asked if she could sing in the chorus just for the Fauré *Requiem.* She said she was crazy about the Fauré *Requiem* and wanted to participate in the rehearsals and performance of just that program. Yes, I remember Juliana Franck. Unusual girl, pretty girl."

"Yes," said Lawrence, imagining the opening phrases of the *Requiem.* Juliana Franck!

"Is she in some kind of trouble?" asked Stein, aware of Lawrence's distraction.

"No trouble," said Lawrence. "I've seen her a couple of times about college, and I wanted to know what kind of musician she is. By the way, did Hilton let her sing in the *Requiem*?"

"Nope—he thought she had a lot of nerve."

"Mm."

Betts Storey had been concerned that the two appointments, scheduled fifteen minutes apart, were unnecessarily close, especially because there was plenty of free time on either side of them. Lawrence assured her the appointments were fine—and that it was not certain the Berrisford boy would even show up. He told Betts to ask them, if and when they arrived, to wait on the bench in the short corridor between her desk and his office.

"If I'm here, I will," said Betts, still visibly bewildered. "But, the way you've got them scheduled, I'll be at lunch when they come."

"That'll be no problem. I'll keep an ear tuned."

When Betts left the guidance wing to go to the cafeteria, Lawrence went to her desk and switched on her intercom, then returned to his office, closed his door, and locked it.

A minute or two after the appointed time, Lawrence heard a questioning "Hello?" over the intercom—Juliana. A few seconds later, another. Then there was a knock on his door.

"Mr. Lawrence! *Mr. Lawrence?*"

Lawrence sat still in his swivel chair, facing a leafless, leaden-gray prospect of lawn, street, and tennis court. He closed his eyes. *It is more than permissible for me to be asleep in here,* he told himself.

Lawrence sat, unmoving and hyper-alert, while Juliana Franck, blanched by the fluorescent lights overhead, waited on the bench outside his office. Twice Lawrence heard retreating footsteps, but each time there was a return to the bench. Maybe I should call her in anyway, he thought. "I'm sorry," he would say. "Have you been here long? I was reading." Yes, Lawrence decided. He would do that. It would be good to see her.

"Oh—" Lawrence heard over the intercom. This voice belonged to Paul. "Is Mr. Lawrence in, do you know?"

"No, he's out. Probably at lunch."

"He asked me to see him at 12:45," said Paul. "Maybe he forgot. You're waiting for him, too?"

"Mm. College."

"College—oh no! The future." Lawrence listened to them laugh.

"Well, you're ahead of me," said Paul. "I should probably

get going. I'm supposed to be in a class sixth period."

"Oh—I don't have a class sixth period. You can go in ahead of me if you like . . . if he ever comes back."

"Do you think he's in there sleeping?" Paul asked. Juliana laughed.

"Or hiding?" she said.

"You know," said Paul, "I really ought to get going . . . in spite of your generous offer."

"Is that *She*?" exclaimed Juliana. "Are you really reading *She*, 'who-must-be-obeyed'?"

"As, um, a matter of fact, yes."

"Oh, Rider Haggard!" said Juliana. "I used to have such a passion for Rider Haggard—when I was about eight."

"Well, I'm afraid that's still about my speed. I read Rider Haggard at least once a year."

"Do you know," said Juliana excitedly—Lawrence, straining not to breathe in order to hear her better, wished he could see Juliana's face as she spoke—"that rereading books is proof of their immortal greatness? C. S. Lewis says that, and I think it's true. Books that are true never wear out."

"So it doesn't mean I have the taste of an eight-year-old?"

"No, the opposite. It means you're a real reader. Have you read *King Solomon's Mines*?" Juliana asked.

"Yes. Everything he wrote."

"That's my favorite, Rider Haggard. Who else do you like?"

There was a silence, then Paul laughed. "I don't think you're ready for this. I'm not your conventional reader. What I actually read most is—" more laughter.

"What?"

"It's another children's book."

"But that's terrific. What?"

"*The Wind in the Willows.*"

"Really? Really! Well, that's terrific. That's perfect."

"So you've obviously read *Wind in the Willows.*"

"I'm always reading it. 'Messing about in boats'? 'The Piper at the Gates of Dawn'? All the *meals*? It's a whole world."

"How about Mr. Toad's driving?"

"Yes! Ah, but he paid for it, didn't he? The prison term, the washerwoman disguise—"

"The capture of Toad Hall—"

"By weasels and stoats."

"Maybe," said Paul, "there are more secret *Wind in the Willows* readers out there than I thought. I mean, you're the first person I ever asked about it, and look, you know everything. So maybe, just below the surface, the students and the *faculty*—"

"Oh, wouldn't it be nice if it was true?" There was a silence. Lawrence strained to hear. Then Juliana said, "Oh, dear," then something muffled, nearly inaudible. "Oh, dear," she said again.

"I wonder," said Paul, "whether it's against the rules to be late for a class because you're waiting for a guidance counselor who's late for an appointment?"

"Oh, that can't possibly be against the rules."

"I don't know," said Paul, adding with exaggerated seriousness, "I might not be taking proper responsibility. But—I guess I'll risk it." Lawrence heard what he assumed was an armload of books crash to the floor.

"Now tell me," Paul continued, "why are you into *Wind in the Willows*? My interest is probably genetic. My mother illustrates children's books for a living, and there've always been thousands of children's books, and children's book pictures, and books about children's books around our house. My mother's book name is Elizabeth Chauncy. That's her maiden name. Have you ever seen any of her books?"

"I think so," said Juliana. "Has she done the illustrations for a series of Hans Christian Andersen tales? Fairly recently?"

"Yes, she does those."

"Oh, they're wonderful! She gets an effect with her colors just like stained glass. Oh, dear. Tell your mother she has an admirer at the high school."

"Okay, I'll tell her. What's her admirer's name?"

"What? Oh, I'm sorry. My name is Juliana Franck. How do you do?"

"'How do I do?' That is the most formal greeting I've ever heard in this school." Juliana made a sound, but Paul cut her short. "No—no, it's nice. It's really nice. I'm Paul Berrisford. I'm a junior. How do you do?"

"Very well, thanks."

"Speaking of pictures," said Paul, "have you ever seen the one in Mr. Lawrence's office, the one with the boy in tights offering a flower to a girl in a long dress?"

"Yes, it was the first thing I saw when I went in there. I like it. I like their serious attitude."

"Yes, they're serious. I like the mood of it, the kind of place they're in. Is it a forest?"

"I don't know. They're alone somewhere, and it's dark."

"I really like it," said Paul. "It takes you back—"

"Well, hello," said Betts Storey. "Are you both waiting for Mr. Lawrence? Isn't he in? Did he go out somewhere?"

"I think he's out," said Juliana. "His office door is locked."

"It is, is it?" said Betts Storey. "Let me just see if there's a message here somewhere . . ." Lawrence felt his heartbeat quicken. "No, I don't see anything. Well, for heaven's sakes, my intercom is on. Mr. Lawrence, Mr. Lawrence—are you there? Anybody there? I just can't imagine where he would—"

"What can I do for you?" Lawrence said over the intercom. "Has either the Franck girl or the Berrisford boy turned up yet?"

"Both of them are right here. They've been waiting for you. It's twenty minutes past one."

"*Really.* Well, send them in, please. Why don't I see Miss Franck first?"

The door to the office opened, and Lawrence stepped out into the hallway. He held a file—Juliana's—in one hand, and his demeanor suggested that he had been roused suddenly from deeply engaging work.

"Hello, Juliana. Hello, Paul. I'm sorry you were out here waiting for me. You should've come to the door."

"I did," said Juliana brightly.

"Did you?" said Lawrence. "Again, I'm sorry."

"It was no problem," said Juliana. "We were talking about great literature and great painting."

"Well, that sounds better than discussing colleges. However, if you still want to talk about college, I'm glad to do so. I can write an admission slip to your next class."

"Oh, I tell you what I think I'll do," said Juliana. "He has a sixth-period class which is already half over. I have a seventh-period class, which I really should not miss. So why not see him now through the rest of the period, and I'll come again sometime when you're free."

"Hey, I don't want to take your—" began Paul.

"You're not. This is fine. You don't want to miss two classes, do you?" she said.

"Oh no, never," he shot back. Laughter.

"I'll see you tomorrow, or sometime soon," said Juliana to Lawrence. She gathered up her books from the bench. Then, to Paul: "It was a pleasure to meet you. Please tell your mother how much I admire her pictures."

"I'll do it."

Juliana left the guidance office, and Lawrence motioned for Paul to lead the way through his door. "See if we can arrange an appointment for Miss Franck during a free period tomorrow," Lawrence said to Betts Storey.

Before he sat down on the two-seater, Paul took a full, long look at *The Swabian Lovers*. The medieval youth's feeling for the maid could not have been more ardent, yet there was something very formal and restrained in his posture, in the delicate way his fingers barely closed over hers.

Paul sat down and grinned happily at Lawrence. "Where does she want to go to college?"

"She's talked about Columbia."

"Columbia? That's in New York, isn't it?"

"Yes."

"And it's sort of high-powered, Ivy League, isn't it?"

"Yes."

"Mm. I can see that. Is she very smart?"

"I think she's quite a good student. Very bright."

"Juliana Franck," said Paul.

"Yes," said Lawrence. "Could we talk about the PSAT exam, which your group takes this coming Tuesday morning?"

"Sure," said Paul, expansively throwing back his arms over the cushions of the two-seater.

He is colored exactly like a peach, Lawrence noted. And he glows.

CHAPTER *Three*

In the course of an exhilaratingly intense sequence of days, which grew into weeks, Lawrence let himself be drawn into a deep friendship with Paul Berrisford and Juliana Franck. The frequent office "appointments" each of them made began to turn more and more incidentally on Paul's aversion to standardized tests and Juliana's preoccupation with Columbia University. Gradually those concerns became ritualistic, even humorous, points of reference in rambling, gossipy sessions between Lawrence and Paul, Lawrence and Juliana, or, sometimes, all three of them.

One free period, and occasionally two, each school day would be given over to "Guidance," as Paul and Juliana had named it in fun. When the soccer season ended, both Paul and Juliana were likely to stop by Lawrence's office for some valedictory words or to share a joke before heading off to some cheerfully aimless explorations together, usually in the environs of the nearby university.

In Lawrence's office, Paul and Juliana would always occupy the cushioned two-seater, Lawrence his Yale University captain's chair. Sometimes they would linger, drinking the last of the Guidance Department coffee, until Betts Storey and the other staff left the building and the afternoon light of early winter began to fail.

It was toward the end of one such afternoon session that Lawrence looked up from the faces of Paul and Juliana to the still figures of *The Swabian Lovers*, then back to Paul and Juliana. "Do you think you two could assume the pose of the couple overhead?" Lawrence asked on a whim, gesturing in the direction of the print. "I've been studying your four respective countenances for over an hour, and I think it just may be possible to recreate a great moment in art."

Paul and Juliana exchanged a glance of delighted surprise. Juliana rose and moved toward the picture. She turned to Lawrence.

"But we're not dressed properly."

"The attitude is ageless," Lawrence said, "and it's the attitude we're after."

Paul rose to his feet and, with his head cocked to see the picture over his shoulder, began to assume the position of the youth in the print. Without a backward glance, Juliana assumed her position. They edged closer to each other, so that their shoulders lightly met. Juliana raised one hand and curled her fingers in a studied manner. Paul took her raised hand in his. Confident now of the pose, both stared blankly outward, suggesting, with what was to Lawrence a striking exactness, the elevated, slightly dazed look of the youth and the maid in the painting.

"Yes," Lawrence began, eyeing the reproduction closely, then looking directly into the intense faces of Paul and Juliana. They were, he knew, the two most beautiful people he had ever seen.

"Yes," he said again. "That's it."

છ

The night they came to see him at the carriage house did not, for some reason, surprise him. The Friday afternoon before Christmas break, Paul and Juliana had stopped by his office to wish him a happy holiday. They had asked if he was going out of town for the break.

Lawrence said no, he never did. Vacations on his own, he told them, not quite truthfully, were his happiest times. Paul had asked him where he lived, and when Lawrence told him the neighborhood and the address, Juliana lit up: "We're practically neighbors! I had no idea."

Lawrence, of course, knew the exact proximity of the Franck house—three and a half blocks, and no more than a five- or six-minute walk away. Lawrence made a light self-deprecatory remark about carriage house renters being something less than full-blooded neighbors.

"We'll come see you," said Paul. "Some night when you're

least expecting it."

"We'll sing you carols," said Juliana.

"By all means," Lawrence had said.

Alix Devereaux did not go out of town for Christmas either, and Lawrence spent the first night of the vacation with her in her northside apartment. They had eaten and drunk a good deal, so much in fact that Lawrence could not recall clearly the transition to lovemaking, which seemed agreeably prolonged and, like the meal, heavy.

At two-thirty a.m., Lawrence awoke clear-headed in Alix's bed. She was asleep, turned away from him, her cheek, rounded shoulder, and back down to her shoulder blades appearing gray-blue and pink from the commercial lighting of the broad avenue beyond her window. Lawrence propped himself up and looked out along the brilliantly lit but empty street. It was snowing.

Lawrence wanted to be home rather than in the comfort of Alix's bed. Home was in the orbit of Paul and Juliana. Alix's was not. He thought of them, aimlessly driving about Evanston, or walking, as he would like to be walking, through the old residential neighborhoods, the snow falling through the quiet in heavy wet flakes. Lawrence wanted to be home by himself, and he wanted Paul and Juliana to come visit him.

Lawrence went home late the next morning. He passed the following two nights by himself, intermittently reading in front of the electric heater the owners had installed in the fire-place opening. As frequently happened to Lawrence on school vacations, he seemed to spend a lot of time in his darkened sitting room. Late and early, waking and sleeping, melded together into a single quality, almost a substance. Lawrence was used to spending long periods of time quietly and entire-ly alone. He rather welcomed it.

Lawrence looked over his pictures and furnishings as if he were a stranger sizing up the invisible occupant of these rooms: the deep roses and blues and golds of two worn Oriental carpets, the engraved views of Oxford colleges and Yale in their gilt frames, the framed prints of Leonardo sketches on the mantel, the darkness and heaviness of the fur-niture. These were definitely a bachelor's rooms. And this bachelor was nothing if not an academic.

Lawrence scanned the walls, the table surfaces, and the open doorway to his bedroom for a sign of something that would place his apartment in the late twentieth century. There is nothing, he thought. No, there was the stereo, its jewel-sized power light glowing at him like a tiny coal from across the darkened room.

At such solitary times, Lawrence's thoughts were likely to turn to the question of whether he "mattered." He had learned to think about the question objectively. A person matters, he decided, to the extent others are affected by him and think about him. *It is unlikely that anyone else thinks about you very much or very deeply,* Lawrence told himself critically. Was it true? Family would think about him, but Lawrence had no family. There had been no family since his parents died, within a year of one another, when he was thirty.

"Tell me we should be doing this," Lawrence heard Juliana say as they climbed the steps.

"We should be doing this," said Paul. "We're all friends."

At the top of the stairs, Lawrence opened the door to greet them.

"Very impressive sleuth work, you two," said Lawrence. "Nobody finds this place."

"No problem," said Paul.

"It was simple," said Juliana, lightly whisking snow flakes out of her hair. "We just came to the first carriage house on the street with you in it."

"Well, I'm glad you did," said Lawrence, taking their coats and scarves.

"Happy Christmas Eve," said Paul.

Lawrence led Paul and Juliana through the little kitchen into the sitting room, which, but for the orange-pink bands of electric fire, was still dark. Lawrence turned on two small table lamps covered by green glass globes.

"Oh, look at this wonderful place," Juliana said to Paul. "It could be right out of Dickens."

"A good bit of it comes right out of the Salvation Army," Lawrence said, gesturing for them to sit down on the sofa facing the electric fire.

Paul and Juliana were rosily flushed in the soft light. A little moisture still shone in their hair. Paul wore an outsized sailing sweater over a turtleneck shirt. Juliana's white knitted sweater rose up under her chin, and her thick, immaculate black hair fell down about her shoulders. Her heavy woolen skirt covered the tops of high leather boots she seemed anxious to unzip and remove.

"May I?" she asked.

"Of course," said Lawrence.

The boots placed on the hearth in front of the electric fire, Juliana resumed her seat next to Paul and tucked her feet beneath her. She leaned a little into him, and he took her hand.

The young couple and the guidance counselor regarded each other in silence for a moment, and then they laughed.

"Okay," said Paul. "So what have you been doing, Mr. Lawrence? How have you been spending your vacation?"

"Would you honestly like to know what a forty-one-year-old bachelor does with his free time?"

"Yes!"

"Yes!"

"All right, then. I'll tell you. Are you sure you're ready for this? It's the truth."

"I'm ready for the truth," said Juliana.

"Well, here it is," Lawrence paused. "Nothing. I've done absolutely nothing. I just sit here in the not quite firelight and think and doze, think and doze, maybe read a little."

"Oh, that sounds perfect."

"No, I tell a lie," Lawrence resumed. "I did do one thing. I did move once from this spot. On Friday, the last day of school, I went to see my friend, Miss Devereaux, in the city. I did that."

"Oh, I love her," said Juliana energetically.

"Miss Devereaux," said Paul. "Yes. I think she's a very beautiful woman."

"A beautiful and accomplished woman," said Lawrence. "And a wonderful cook."

There was a pause. Then Paul resumed: "And you've been home since Friday, just sitting still and thinking, all right here?"

"That's it exactly."

"God, I admire that," said Paul warmly. "Nobody does that and admits it. It's just the way I would like to spend my time, if I could."

"*Paul,*" began Juliana in surprise. "I've never seen you sit still quietly or for a minute."

Paul grinned. "I know you haven't, and I may never. I hate

time."

Lawrence suddenly thought of Paul's PSAT test, its randomly blacked-in circles at the end of the verbal section, and the answerless mathematics grid.

"You said you were reading, too," Juliana continued. "Tell me something. This is important to me. Were you reading new things or rereading old ones?"

Lawrence reflected. What *had* he read? He had read St. Mark's Gospel in the King James Version. He had read Longus's romance *Daphnis and Chloe* (great pleasure), and he had dipped in and out of Mark Helprin's *Winter's Tale*. He had also pulled his Modern Library Keats from its place and was on the brink of reading "The Eve of St. Agnes" again.

"Rereading," said Lawrence. "I've never really thought about it, but I guess rereading is all the reading I do."

"That's just it!" Juliana exclaimed. "The rereading is proof, you see—" She looked excitedly at Paul and cupped his shoulder in her hand. "We talk about this a lot. The rereading is proof that what the stories say is really true. Really true stories never wear out. You can get tired of them for a bit, but then when you're rested, you come right back to them, the real ones. It's true of movies, too. Now, tell me—and I should have asked this first—what were you rereading?"

Lawrence told her.

"Oh," said Juliana. "That's perfect. Except I don't know

that *Winter's Tale*, and I don't know *Daphnis and Chloe*, except the musical one."

"I recommend both. In fact . . ." Lawrence rose and went into his bedroom, where he picked up two books from a stack on his night table. "Here they are. Read them. Both of you. Take your time. They're definite rereads."

"Are you sure?"

"Absolutely. A Christmas present from your guidance counselor."

Paul and Juliana each opened a book and began to read.

"Paul," Lawrence interrupted, "I have something I want you to hear."

Lawrence moved across to his bookshelves, where his records were lined upright. He hunched down before them and drew some of the records forward from the line. "You play the guitar, right? The acoustic guitar?"

"Mm."

"Do you play blues?"

"Yeah, I think."

"Well, here are some blues. Here are the beginning and essence of the blues. Juliana," Lawrence said, crossing to the stereo with a handful of record albums, "do you know this music?"

"Oh, I don't think so. Probably not."

"It might sound very jangling and crude to you, but listen

for a minute, because there's something behind it." Lawrence placed a disc on the turntable. "This first bit is an old recording from an old tape. It's a Southern blues player named Robert Johnson. After you get the gist of that, I want to put on an interpretation of the same tune by a young white player named John Hammond." Lawrence looked to Paul for a sign of recognition, but there was none. Lawrence placed the tone arm onto the record, producing a quiet hiss. Paul and Juliana sat back on the sofa.

Lawrence wondered why, when played for ears other than his own, that his stereo sounded with unearthly brilliance and clarity, as if the entire room were somehow a speaker and the pulsing thumps and whines of Robert Johnson's guitar were forming themselves spontaneously all about them. The black man's voice sounded as Lawrence hoped it would—a husky, imploring moan, broken by little falsetto cries:

I'm gonna drive slow and easy, girl.
Any way to make it last,
Yes, I'm gonna drive slow and easy,
Any way to make it last.

The "Terraplane Blues" ended with a bent, sharp blue note, and Lawrence lifted the tone arm.

"That's fine," said Paul.

"Now listen to what happens when it comes up north and into a real recording studio." Lawrence set the tone arm down on the "Terraplane Blues" band of the John Hammond recording. Everything was richer, fuller, and more gleamingly metallic. But the white man's voice captured some of the black man's seductive cooing and moaning. The fuller, slower treatment of the song seemed to hold it, still and mournful, above their heads.

"That's fine, too," said Paul when it was over.

"Oh, Paul, would you play?" Juliana hooked her arm under Paul's. "Please play." Then, to Lawrence: "You should really hear Paul play. I've never heard anything like it."

"I'd like that very much," said Lawrence, a little startled. "Have you got an instrument nearby?"

"He does."

"My guitar's in the car, down the street. But I'm doing fine here. I'd like to hear some more of your blues stuff. Those two guys are new to me."

"I'll be glad to play you some more," said Lawrence. "I think I own the entire history of the blues, but if you don't mind, I'd really like to hear you play."

"Go get your guitar, Paul," Juliana urged. Paul rose to his feet and headed coatless out the kitchen door.

"Wait till you hear," said Juliana, rearranging herself on the sofa. In the silence that followed Paul's departure, she added, "It's such a beautiful guitar."

It *was* a beautiful guitar. The body of the instrument was lacquered in a brilliant sunburst pattern, and in the fretted fingerboard were laid Indian totems in mother-of-pearl. Even as he withdrew it from the plush burgundy interior of its case, Paul was at once careful and comfortable with the instrument. Seated on the floor with his back against the sofa, he bent solicitously over the guitar body and tuned it, testing each adjustment with sharply strummed chords. Then there was a rapidly executed, tinkling run. "Okay," he said, baring his prominent, slightly bucked teeth in a smile that was at once self-conscious and inviting.

"Play 'Candy Man,'" Juliana urged.

Paul grinned again, and then threw his head back to clear the shock of hair that had fallen over his forehead.

"I don't know," he said. "It's a bawdy song, and we're here with our guidance counselor."

"Yes," Lawrence said with mock gravity, and they laughed.

"It isn't a bawdy song," said Juliana. "It's a wonderful song. Is it really a bawdy song, Paul?"

She could be a child of ten, Lawrence thought to himself.

"It's bawdy, I'm afraid," said Paul.

"I think we're up to it," said Lawrence. "Let's hear it."

Paul flashed them a quick look, a look suggesting that he

was in possession of a surprising secret, and then he bent low over the guitar and began to play. He established a jumpy, staccato rhythm with his thumb, over which he picked out an unexpectedly pleasing melody. Whereas the stereo playing had held a place in the room, Paul's guitar filled it.

Paul had strong, large hands, sharp, prominent wrist bones, long fingers, and sharply jointed thumbs. His playing was sure. Bass line and melody combined and recombined in varied syncopations. There was a brightness about the sound, almost the quality of moving water. Without looking up, Paul began to sing softly.

All you good ladies gather round,
The good sweet candy man's in town,
He's candy,
Yes, a candy man.
Now don't stand close to the candy man,
He'll leave a stick of candy in your hand.
He's candy,
Yes, he's a candy man.

It was an extraordinary voice, Lawrence thought. It began somewhere deep in the throat, almost as a murmur. There was a childlike quality about it—or perhaps the deeper expression of the childlike qualities of the boy himself. There was a slight over-elaboration of his diction as he half-sang, half-whispered the words, which created the impression that he was imparting something private and important.

Juliana inclined toward him in concentration. As he listened, Lawrence himself felt tingling along his spine. It occurred to him that Paul was probably not striving for an effect in his playing. This was the boy himself. When Paul finished, Juliana and Lawrence at once demanded more.

Paul dropped his gaze, adjusted his position, bent over his guitar again, and began to play. There were similar, subtly complex embellishments of nursery tunes, standard folk songs, a Beatles song or two, and even some show tunes. Paul played and sang for over an hour without stopping, each song, even the most familiar, transformed by his unusual voice, which could whisper, sustain delicately, or bark huskily, as the lyrics required.

Paul stopped suddenly and swept the hair away from his forehead. "Well, you've heard me now," he said, eyes wide, a little embarrassed.

"I'm glad we did. You're very good, Paul. And that's not a polite opinion. You *are* very good."

"That was wonderful, Paul. Thank you for doing it," said Juliana. Then, turning to Lawrence: "Do you realize how hard it is to get him to play? He never plays for people, except audiences. I cannot get him to play for my family."

"Her family are real musicians," said Paul.

"You are a real musician," said Juliana.

Lawrence noted again the beauty of the guitar, now standing upright against the fireplace. The lacquered wood grain, giving way to honey and rose, was strangely continuous with Paul himself, with his straw-and-honey-colored hair, with the burst of his toothy grin.

"Oh," Juliana said suddenly. "Paul, play your song. The one you wrote."

Genuine self-consciousness now: Paul looked pleadingly up at Juliana on the sofa. "No. Hey. That's really . . . out of the way."

"Oh no it isn't," said Juliana warmly, meeting the directness of Paul's gaze. Lawrence felt himself briefly eclipsed by the intensity of their communion. "Please play it. Please? This one more thing, and then I promise to stop with the requests."

From where he sat, Indian-style, Paul made a slow-motion punching gesture up toward Juliana, who dipped her head to meet it. As his hand touched her cheek, it opened and he ran his finger lightly down the side of her face and neck.

"You," he said to her.

Paul then retrieved his guitar and positioned himself to play. He looked up to Lawrence and said, "I don't know how to explain this one. It's kind of a children's song, I guess."

"It isn't a children's song," said Juliana softly.

Paul played a descending progression of rich minor chords and sang.

I found a little girl in a land without trees,
I picked her up and took her out of time.
She grew tall and strong there in my cottage in the woods
And when she was a woman she was mine.

She grew tall and strong there in my cottage by the lake,
We'd lie in the shade of the trees.
And though her mouth was laughing and she smiled with her eyes,
I could sense a sadness singing in the leaves.

One day she went out walking
And I fell far behind,
Her mouth and eyes were laughing
But mine were full of tears.
I heard her footfalls up ahead.
Then there were only mine.
Stay with me, I think she said,
But it's been many years.
So soon her footsteps disappeared and there were only mine,
I looked and saw the land was in a freeze.
A frozen lifetime later I recognized the road,
The path into the land without trees,

The path into the land without trees.

"Thank you," Juliana said when he finished.

"Enough from me," Paul said exuberantly. He sprang to his feet and stretched. "Poor you," he said to Lawrence. "You got the whole show."

"Poor me, nothing," Lawrence said. "The show could've gone on longer. Paul, really. You have a terrific talent. I'm even kind of a folk snob. You've got a quality—in your singing and playing—that's not like anybody else's. I've never heard anything like it."

"You're an original!" said Juliana.

"Get her," said Paul, bending forward to touch his toes. "She's the only real musician I've ever met, and she likes asking me to get out my toy guitar. You should hear her play, Mr. Lawrence. Her cello. Now, that's a sound. That takes you right back. Have you ever heard her?"

"No," said Lawrence. "But I'd like to."

"Any evening in the Franck parlor," Juliana said. "Stop by at any time, for any reason, and you'll get unlimited hours of quartets, trios, duets, even symphonies if the relatives are over."

"She jokes about it," said Paul. "But you should hear her. She can really play." To Juliana: "You and your cello, Jewel, are one thing."

Jewel. Lawrence had heard Paul use this diminutive before and had always assumed it was "Jule." But it was "Jewel." Juliana *was* a jewel.

As he offered the two a late-night snack of ham sandwiches and tea, Lawrence also learned that she was Jewish.

Both of them, after polite demurrals, had enthusiastically accepted Lawrence's offer—he had but one lone packet of Danish ham. They had moved into the kitchen, when Paul asked Juliana, "Can you have ham sandwiches?"

"Why can't she?" said Lawrence, nosing into the refrigerator for some lettuce. "Has she heard something about my kitchen standards?"

Then, just as the realization that Juliana was Jewish formed itself clearly in Lawrence's mind, Paul said, "Isn't it a sin?"

"No," said Juliana, near laughter. "It isn't a sin. I'm not Orthodox, and the Francks don't keep kosher."

"So it's all right to eat ham?"

"Well, not exactly all right. We're really not supposed to eat ham, except in dire life-threatening emergencies. I can't actually imagine a life-threatening emergency that could be relieved by ham. But there are times when a lapse is forgivable. At least, I can forgive myself for a periodic lapse of ham. Now I'm going to have to stop talking about eating ham, or else I won't be able to eat it."

"Why don't I make you something else?" Lawrence asked,

aware that the absence of actual alternatives had possibly undermined any graciousness in his tone. "Perhaps a nice . . . egg sandwich? I see there's an egg here." Lawrence eyed the single egg in the egg carton. He could not remember buying eggs in weeks, maybe months.

"No, the ham is fine," insisted Juliana. "When in Babylon . . ."

"When in *Babylon*?" Paul asked.

"It's a reference from religion and history," said Juliana. The kettle whistled. "There goes the hot water. Let's make a lot of tea. One cup is never enough tea. I could drink gallons of tea in the winter."

There, in the too white light of his kitchen, Lawrence was happier than at any other time he could remember. Paul and Juliana, even in their instinctive restraint and courtesy, were wholly in love. They stole looks at each other, occasionally letting their mutual gaze come to rest. There was something almost languid, something out-of-time about their movements around one another, about their casual talk. They were in love, and Lawrence somehow felt included in it.

Lawrence toasted six slices of wheat bread, spread them with a thin layer of butter, daubed on mustard, laid down a water-limp lettuce leaf on each slice, added a sleek and gelatinous slice of packaged ham, and closed the sandwiches. He put each on a plate, placed a dill gherkin to one side, and, gripping two of the plates with his right hand, moved back to the sitting room. Juliana followed with tea and mugs on a tray.

"Oh, let's do one thing," said Juliana as they seated themselves again. "Let's turn out the lamps and have only the fireplace."

"I'm afraid it's not a crackling blaze out of Dickens," said Lawrence, who was nonetheless happy to comply.

"It'll be fine," said Juliana. "There, isn't this perfect?"

The radiation of orange, pink, and pale blue from the electric heater lit only an oval of carpet in front of the hearth. The irregular glow was reflected in the sheen of dishes, the gilt corners of picture frames, the glass decanters on the sideboard. Apart from the fireplace, the only bead of light came from the stereo's ruby red power signal.

Juliana raised a ceramic mug to her lips with both hands and sipped some tea.

Paul, Lawrence noted with interest, had, without haste or sloppiness, eaten his sandwich and pickle already, seemingly in an instant.

"May I get you something else, Paul?" Lawrence asked. The image of the solitary egg rose to consciousness.

"Oh, no thanks," Paul said. "I'm fine. I'm also bottomless."

"I'd offer you half of mine," said Juliana, smiling, "but this is the best ham sandwich I've ever eaten. Mr. Lawrence is a genius."

"Yes, the culinary standards here are very high," Lawrence said.

Lawrence felt himself growing uneasy in the lovely light, and he identified the source of his feeling almost at once: it was getting late, and Paul and Juliana would want to leave soon.

"There's more music, you know," he said, crossing to his records. "There's some very important music, and it must be played in this particular light or not at all."

"More blues?" asked Paul.

"Nope," said Lawrence. "This is even sadder than the blues. But much more beautiful."

"What?" said Juliana, full of interest.

"This needs just a bit of explaining," Lawrence began. "The text is kind of mysterious, but it's very haunting. It's not the kind of thing you'll easily forget. Here's the background.

"At Oxford University, back in the 1600s, a young scholar tired of academic life and began taking an interest in gypsies. Whether the appeal was gypsy mysteries or getting out of Oxford is not known, but the boy left his friends and took to the road. Afterward, for years, then for centuries, there would be reports of 'The Scholar-Gypsy' spotted somewhere—crossing a country bridge or waking early in a farmer's field. Legend had it that because the scholar's wandering quest for gypsy meaning was pure, he never changed and never aged. Are you with me so far?"

"Right with you," said Paul quickly.

"And the story's been set to music?" Juliana asked.

"Yes, it has. But first it was made into a longish poem by Matthew Arnold. Do you know him?" Lawrence asked.

"Afraid not," said Paul.

"'Dover Beach,'" said Juliana.

"That's the one," Lawrence continued. "A Victorian. Arnold wrote two poems that touched on the Scholar-Gypsy story. One is called 'The Scholar-Gypsy,' the other is called 'Thyrsis,' and they're both about the loss of a friend Arnold loved. The lost, dead friend was a questing, pure sort of soul who left the dried-up academic world to wait, and now I'm quoting, for 'the spark from heaven to fall.'" Lawrence paused. "Are you still with me? Is this too much like a class?"

Paul and Juliana appeared to be raptly attentive to what he had been saying. Lawrence found that he had even stirred himself a little by the force of his narration. He looked across the darkness to Paul and Juliana seated, shoulder-to-shoulder, arm in arm, on the sofa.

"This is wonderful," Juliana said. "Keep going."

"There's not much more. Except that an English composer, Ralph Vaughan Williams . . ." Lawrence paused again to see if Juliana showed any sign of recognition . . . "Ralph Vaughan Williams composed this dreamy piece, mixing together bits of

'Scholar-Gypsy' and 'Thyrsis'. Some bits are sung, some recited. It's an amazing musical treatment of written poetry. I'm tempted to have you read the words from the record jacket, but that would require more light, and I think we've got the ideal scholar-gypsy light in the room right now."

"No, let's just listen," said Juliana.

"Right," said Lawrence. "Here goes. The whole piece is called *Oxford Elegy*. Ready?" Lawrence lowered the tone arm onto the record.

His longstanding love of the piece had been so intensified by his preamble that Lawrence felt an almost unpleasant pitch of arousal when the boys' chorus began its ascending, wordless swirls. Lawrence felt over-stimulated, tingling, drugged. At the narrator's first words, *Go, for they call you shepherd, from the hill,* Lawrence reclined on the floor in front of the hearth and closed his eyes.

He may have slept intermittently. He did not, he knew, hear the sequence of sung, spoken, and orchestral passages of *Oxford Elegy* as they were performed. There were instead brilliantly colored word-pictures: two-dimensional images more jewel-bright than stained glass. In fact, the images appeared as if through a window or a frame, as if, from a dark space, darker than the room, he could look into still scenes of unearthly vividness. He could picture the wooly backs of sheep:

Cross and recross the strips of moon blanch'd green
Then the dazzling white-yellows of high summer.
Through the thick corn, the scarlet poppies peep,
And round green roots and yellowing stalks I see
Pale pink convolvulus in tendrils creep.

Then a prospect of Oxford on the summer horizon:
That sweet city with her dreaming spires.
Then a river, a wide quiet river parting a green expanse of meadow:
Or in my boat I lie
Moor'd to the cool bank in the summer heats.

Then winter, cold, driving winter—and a glimpse of the Scholar-Gypsy in his tattered black:

Wrapt in thy cloak and battling with the snow . . .
Turn'd once to watch while thick the snowflakes fall,
The line of festal light in Christ Church hall.

More whirls and wisps of lush verdure, then its aching absence.

. . . I wander'd till I died. Roam on!
The light we sought is shining still.
Our tree yet crowns the hill,

Our scholar travels yet the loved hillside.

The record ended. Lawrence sat up suddenly.

"And there you have it."

"Oh, Mr. Lawrence," said Juliana, inclining herself forward and closing her eyes. "Mr. Lawrence, that was magical. That whole story is the saddest, sweetest thing I've ever heard. Oh. What is it called? *The Scholar-Gypsy,* by Vaughan Williams? It's one of those things I have to own forever."

"It's called *An Oxford Elegy.* 'The Scholar-Gypsy' is one of the poems by Matthew Arnold."

"Yes, I want those, too. Oh, Paul," she said, turning to him, "did you love it?"

"You know," said Paul, "it's funny. I was never sure I was following along, that I was getting it, but I did get it. I really did, if the main thing is that the scholar-gypsy is gone, but never really gone."

"That's it," said Lawrence. "That's the idea." Then, to Juliana: "So you really liked it? I'm glad. It's a tricky business playing things you're crazy about for other people. It can be the very food of your soul, but other people can just glaze over with boredom."

"Oh no," Juliana said energetically. "No boredom. That piece is one of the most important things that's happened to me this year. I have to buy it now."

"Well, until you do, please take this one on loan." Lawrence inserted the record into its sleeve and handed it to Juliana.

"Oh, I couldn't," she said, taking it. "This is your treasure."

"No, please. It's just a loan. And I've got *Oxford Elegy* in deep, permanent storage. Nothing could give me more pleasure than your falling under the sway of 'The Scholar-Gypsy' and Vaughan Williams."

"Paul," Juliana said, tugging at his elbow and smiling. "Look at what we've got. These magical books"—Juliana thumped the jackets of *Daphnis and Chloe* and *Winter's Tale*— and now this music. I cannot believe this evening."

"Hey, Jewel," Paul said, clasping her shoulders and shaking her slowly from side to side. "I'll bet Mr. Lawrence might want to turn in. Don't you think?"

Juliana closed her eyes tight. "No, I don't think."

"What time do you think it is?" Paul asked Lawrence.

"I'm afraid to look."

"Mm."

"If I weren't your responsible, middle-aged guidance counselor, I'd help you with a scheme to explain the hour, but how can I do that? I'll be happy to take the blame, however, if that would help."

Juliana yawned. "Oh, dear. Why are we always in this spot?"

"Seriously, this is my thoughtlessness," said Lawrence. "Let me talk to your folks. Are you going to be in trouble?" Lawrence stole a look at his watch—it was twenty-five minutes past two. "Oh, dear."

"I'm okay," said Paul. "My parents have sort of given up. They basically want me to come home at the end."

"Is that also the Franck policy?" Lawrence asked.

"No, I'm afraid it isn't. The Franck policy is to return at the 'stated time.' Tonight the stated time was one. What were we doing at one?"

"Ham sandwiches," said Paul.

"Right! I think I'll skip the account of those. No, the fault is mine. I knew it was late. I knew it and I didn't care. I wanted to stay here forever."

Lawrence led Paul and Juliana to their coats and waited by the kitchen door as they put them on. Paul went back to the sitting room for his guitar.

"You know," Juliana said to Lawrence, "you have what I consider to be the perfect life. You have this wonderful little house completely to yourself, with all the things in it you love. And you can do whatever you want. I mean, tomorrow, you can sleep late if you want, and read whatever you want. You seem so free, so connected to so many good things."

"Do you think I'm freer than you?"

"Much freer."

"I wonder," said Lawrence.

"Mr. Lawrence, thanks. We really barged in on you. We ate your ham . . ."

"Thank you, Paul . . . for the concert and for your company. You two are the best company in Illinois."

Paul threw an arm around Juliana's shoulders.

"Here," said Lawrence. "Let me take you down the inside stairway. The outside steps get icy." Lawrence led Paul and Juliana down into the three-car garage, which was once the main garage of the big house.

"Hey, what's this?" Paul asked, pointing at an automobile, visible mainly in silhouette.

"Ah, that," said Lawrence. "That's my car."

"I thought you told us once you didn't drive," said Juliana.

"I don't. I can drive, and I do own this ancient car, but not, alas, a current license plate."

"What is it?" asked Paul, obviously interested.

"It's a 1960 Renault Dauphine. Probably the only one extant in the world, certainly the only one of its color. Here. You have to see this." Lawrence moved to the wall and switched on the garage lights.

"Oh, my," said Juliana. "That *is* an unusual car. It's sort of the color of cheese."

"My late father," said Lawrence, "described the color once as 'cold vomit'. Pardon the vulgarity, but it *is* a striking description."

"It looks in great shape," said Paul, peering inside.

"It is, I think. Every few months, I start it and drive it a little. I'm mainly keeping it for its sculptural qualities. I bought it for $150 from a friend when I was in college. It's the only car I've ever liked, although I don't care much for driving."

"That's another absolutely perfect thing you have," said Juliana. "You're amazing."

"Juliana, I think you may be the first and only person I've ever amazed. I think the consensus around the campus is that old Mr. Lawrence is pretty dull. Drive home safely, you two. It's slippery out there. Please blame me for everything. And thanks for the visit."

"Happy Christmas, Mr. Lawrence!"

Juliana blew him a kiss.

CHAPTER *Four*

Lawrence did not see Paul and Juliana again over the holiday break, nor did he expect to. That single visit was somehow sufficient. His contact with them had been more than "professional" for weeks, but now, because they had visited him away from the high school, in his own residence, he felt a genuinely personal basis to their acquaintance.

More important, from his standpoint, Lawrence had a surplus of new images upon which to reflect during his stillest hours. Paul and Juliana newly arrived and dusted with snow on his kitchen stoop. Juliana and Paul nestled into his old sofa in the near darkness. Paul bent quietly over his guitar. Juliana raising her tea mug with both hands. Juliana's face lowered to meet Paul's opening hand. Juliana as "Jewel." "I want to stay here forever." "You have the perfect life." "Mr. Lawrence, you're amazing." The vacation, as he recalled it, was otherwise damp and relentlessly cold.

He had wondered uneasily how they, Juliana especially, had accounted for their late return. At one point he was about to call the Francks to explain that he had been entertaining the pair and to apologize for letting the time get away from them. Then he balked. What if, for some reason, they had told their parents another story, perhaps making no mention of their visit to him? In that case, his call would make more trouble for both of them. Then, too, Lawrence reflected, parents might well have serious reservations about their teenage children spending long, late hours with a guidance counselor who was a middle-aged bachelor.

Lawrence's apprehension came sharply to a head when Betts Storey told him through the intercom that Mr. William Berrisford was on the line and wanted to speak with him.

"Should I tell him you're in?" she asked.

"Yes, I'm in," Lawrence said.

Over the telephone, William Berrisford, Paul's father, instantly made a bluff, though friendly impression. He announced that he had a couple of concerns about Paul. The first was the general lack of drive and focus in his schoolwork, and a so-so performance in his academic courses (he saw little or no work taken home from school). Second, there were his standardized test scores, which were a "disaster." Paul had been "the family flake" since he was a baby, but now things were beginning to count, to have an effect on his future choices. Did Lawrence agree?

Lawrence told Mr. Berrisford that Paul was an interesting and talented boy who, he believed, would have attractive choices after high school. Paul's approach to standardized tests, Lawrence agreed, was a problem that had to be

addressed. It was not, however, a problem related to his aptitude.

"And of course there's this new girl," Berrisford said. "He
seems completely preoccupied with her these days. He's with
her at all hours. Seems a nice enough girl, an attractive girl,
but she's kind of a strange one. She seems to have a complete
hold on him. Is this what you see? Paul says you know her, that
they see you a lot."

"Yes, I know her. Juliana Franck. She's a college ad—"

"Paul told us they've spent some time at your place. There
was one very late evening, wasn't there?"

Perhaps the Berrisfords had not "given up" monitoring
Paul's hours after all, Lawrence said to himself.

"Yes. They did pay me a call over Christmas vacation, and
they did stay late. That was my fault. I was on a kind of vacation night-owl schedule myself. I'm afraid I paid no attention
to the time."

"Not a big issue. We try to let Paul plan his own time,
which worked for his sisters, but he seems for some reason or
other to be out all the time. Maybe we need to pull in the
reins. The only reason I bring up the night at your place is that
the girl's mother phoned Liz—my wife—and was beside herself. They sound as though they're more worried about this
new . . . relationship than we are."

"You're also worried about the relationship?" Lawrence

probed.

"No. Yes. We're worried about Paul. He's a sweet kid, but he doesn't seem connected to reality at all. His mother sees a lot more in him than I do."

"Are you chiefly concerned that he's doing a bad job in school and that he won't have good college prospects?"

"That, among other things. He's just so far away from being an adult. You should see his room. Even if we give him money, he won't buy himself clothes or look after the ones he's got. He won't take care of the car we let him use, and if it breaks down and we don't step in, he's just as glad to get around on foot or to ride his bike over the ice. And he loses everything. Except his guitar. He takes care of that. I'll tell you, if we weren't absolutely certain otherwise, I'd suspect drugs."

"I don't suspect drugs," Lawrence said. "Not in the least."

"Can you imagine this one going off to college?" asked Berrisford.

"It's hard, isn't it?" Lawrence said. "I don't think Paul can imagine going off to college, either."

"That's right. Look, I don't want to take up a lot of your time. I think his mother and I would like to set up an appointment to see you fairly soon. To make a plan and to get your reading. Now, is boarding school a place for a boy like this?"

Lawrence hesitated. "Not necessarily. Why don't you and

Mrs. Berrisford settle on a time when you can both come in, and we'll talk then. You can phone in the day and the time to Mrs. Storey, the Guidance Department secretary."

That next week both Paul and Juliana were distracted and morose.

"They're talking about making him go away to boarding school," Juliana told Lawrence unhappily. "They must think I'm driving him to ruin."

"I think they're worried about him generally," said Lawrence. "I can't imagine that they disapprove of you."

"Oh, they don't say it. They're always very nice. But, underneath, I think Mrs. Berrisford is terrified of me. Do you think they'll send him away to boarding school?"

"I don't know. They haven't really discussed it with me. Personally, I hope not," said Lawrence.

Juliana smiled. "I bet he wouldn't go. I bet he'd disappear."

"Well, I hope he doesn't do that, either. You'd lose him that way too, you know."

"Maybe not," teased Juliana. "Maybe I'd disappear with him."

William and Elizabeth Berrisford, seated before Lawrence on the two-seater, were handsome people. William Berrisford had his son's natural high color. His hair was sandy and brushed across his head from a side part. Only some detectable thickening about the neck and middle suggested that he was old enough to be the parent of grown children.

Elizabeth Berrisford was striking. Lawrence felt himself drawn to her, as if she bore a hard-to-specify likeness to her son. What was it? She was beautiful in a classical, fine-boned way. Her dark, graying hair was pulled up loosely into a bun, one side of which fell away in wisps. Perhaps that was it: the carelessness, which, like Paul's, somehow enhanced her attractiveness. Later, when she became animated in conversation, Lawrence saw what it was. It was a volatile, high-spirited energy, a childlike directness beneath the apparent sophistication. She did not so much resemble Paul, Lawrence realized, as she did Juliana.

"It's not getting any better," William Berrisford was saying. "He lives in a dream."

"He really doesn't do anything harmful or wrong," Elizabeth Berrisford added. "But he's more unreliable and harder to pin down than ever. He's always gone his own way, but now I think he's avoiding us. I think he's mad at his father for bringing up the subject of boarding school."

"I told him—and please don't take this the wrong way—I

told him there were other kinds of schools than this one; that because he was unmotivated in this school did not mean that he would be unmotivated in, say, a first-class boarding school like St. Paul's or Andover," William Berrisford said.

Elizabeth Berrisford looked troubled.

"Mr. Berrisford," Lawrence asked, "what do you think happens in a boarding school?"

"What happens? You mean the difference? Well, there are going to be more high achieving kids per capita. There'll be closer supervision, more attention—I imagine these are the things all the tuition money goes for."

"And you think Paul needs closer supervision and more classroom attention."

"I think he needs something."

"I'm not sure about the boarding school idea at all," said Elizabeth Berrisford. "I'd like to look at it as a kind of last resort. Both Bill and I went away to school, and it was fine, but that was then. I understand boarding schools are very different now. The real issue, I think, is Paul and this girl. We've seen a great deal of her, or we did until a few weeks ago—and she's a lovely person. It's just that she seems to have this spell over Paul. He's bright and alive to anything that has to do with her, but he's an absolute cipher when he's with us. I'm very worried about him."

"And from what we hear from them," Mr. Berrisford

added, "the Francks have many of the same concerns about their daughter. They are a very tightly knit family, I understand."

"Well, really, let's be direct," said Elizabeth Berrisford. "Paul has told me that they don't know what to make of this ever-present, towheaded Gentile boy in their midst. Paul is definitely a guitar, and they are definitely a string ensemble."

"Are you concerned that Juliana is Jewish?" Lawrence asked.

"Not at all."

"Absolutely not."

There was an uncomfortable pause.

"Mr. Lawrence," Mr. Berrisford resumed, somewhat more formally, "you see a fair amount of Paul. Don't you see him once or more a week? He says he drops in whenever his schedule permits."

"Yes, I see Paul most days," said Lawrence. "I also see Juliana Franck."

"Then you have a pretty clear idea how he's performing and what he's thinking about."

Lawrence said nothing.

Mr. Berrisford continued, "Do you see a problem?"

"Something wrong, or something that's blocking Paul's development? No, I don't think I do—which doesn't mean that you don't or that there isn't some kind of a problem. But you asked me honestly, and from my perspective, I'm answering honestly. I think Paul is a distinctive boy, even a bit eccentric, but I don't see him as a problem—except when he sits down to take a standardized test."

Mrs. Berrisford smiled. Mr. Berrisford did not.

"So you don't really see anything to be concerned about in Paul's progress here," said Mr. Berrisford evenly.

"Mr. Berrisford, I can tell you're concerned," said Lawrence, inclining toward them. "But I've told you what I think. Paul is Paul. Now, in addition, he's met a girl he's crazy about, and she's crazy about him. There's the old song that says, 'You're not sick, you're just in love.' I think that's it. It's not a trivial thing. I think it can be a very serious thing, even with teenagers. But it's not a pathology. It's not a problem to be solved."

"So our son is in love at sixteen—."

"Seventeen," Elizabeth Berrisford corrected.

"Our son is in love at seventeen, and we should just resign ourselves to that and let it run its course."

"Love tends to run its course whatever we do," said Lawrence. "But you don't have to resign yourselves to it. Your job, as I understand it, is to behave like parents."

"And how is that, Mr. Lawrence? How should parents behave when someone like Paul starts drifting out of their lives because he's in love? What are you suggesting we should do?"

"I have no suggestions there. Except to do what your feelings as parents tell you to do. I'm not a parent myself. I have no expertise whatsoever. I can sympathize with your frustration, though. I really can. But I also ought to tell you that I admire you both. You've produced a remarkable and talented son. I mean that. I wouldn't lose heart."

"Oh, we won't do that. We just want to make sure we don't lose Paul," said Mrs. Berrisford.

"Thank you, Mr. Lawrence," said Paul's father. "We should probably stay in touch."

With mounting fatigue, Lawrence had just scanned the computer printout of the ninth-graders' Differential Aptitude Test scores when Paul knocked on the frame of his open door.

"Come in, Paul."

"My parents were in yesterday afternoon, weren't they? What's up?"

"I don't know if anything is up. They're feeling way out of touch with you and they're concerned about that."

"*Out of touch?*" Paul flopped down on the two-seater. "I was born out of touch. I don't know when we were ever in touch."

Juliana appeared in the doorway.

"Ah, there you are," she said, moving towards Paul. "I should've known you'd be seeking guidance. Hello, Mr. Lawrence. Tell me about Paul's future. Is he going to be shipped away because he was ruined by that cunning Jewish girl from across town?"

"Yes," said Lawrence. "I've recommended a fine little school for him in the Falkland Islands."

Juliana laughed. "Too close," she said. "I'll find him there."

"Did they sound serious about boarding school?" Paul asked Lawrence.

"I don't think they know. Did they sound serious to you? They're your parents. Have you talked about it at all with them?"

"This is all such a joke," said Paul. "I'm not going to any boarding school."

"You didn't answer my question," Lawrence persisted. "Did you talk to your parents about why they came in?"

"We're not great talkers. They just told me they came in."

"What do you think they're concerned about?" Lawrence asked.

"That I'll be a failure, that I won't get into a classy college, that I'll grow up odd and embarrass them."

"They're concerned about me!" Juliana said. "They're worried that he'll end up with me."

"They're not worried about you," Paul protested. "They like

you. They wish your brainy influence would rub off on me a little."

"You know, Paul," Lawrence said, "your parents are worried about your relationship with Juliana. That's not the same thing as disapproving of her."

"What are they worried about, that I'll be too happy?"

"I don't think they see you enough or talk with you enough to know if you're happy or not."

"Oh, come on . . ."

"Paul, I'm going to talk to you now like a guidance counselor, okay? Is keeping your distance from your parents and breezing through your schoolwork so important to you that you'd let Juliana pay the price?"

"You lost me."

"I mean," continued Lawrence, "that if you could put some effort into your schoolwork and open up a bit to your parents, they'd have less to fear from Juliana and could start to relax about you. That would be much nicer for Juliana—and much fairer. Do you see what I mean?"

"Yeah, I see what you mean," said Paul, enervated.

"On the other hand," continued Lawrence, "if you absolutely need to maintain your swashbuckling independence, you shouldn't mind the modest sacrifice of going off to a boarding school."

"To Falklands Academy."

"Yes, to the St. Falklands School, which would of course leave Juliana free to make her way in New York City, where guitar-playing swashbucklers stand at every street corner."

"Mr. Lawrence, you are poison!" shrieked Juliana.

"For heaven's sake, Paul, go home and be a good boy," Lawrence said lightly.

❧

In the midst of a weighty bundle of Guidance Department mail, Lawrence was surprised to find an invitation from the Berrisfords for dinner and drinks at the North Shore Marina. The impression he had formed over the telephone and on the basis of their single conference was that William Berrisford was critical of him and of the school. There was a restless edge to the questions he had asked, and an impatience with Lawrence's explanations.

He was less sure how he had impressed Elizabeth Berrisford, or if he had made any impression at all. During the conference, she had seemed at once more engaged than her husband but less vocal. She was also, Lawrence recalled, very beautiful.

Because he wondered why the Berrisfords might want to see him socially, he let Paul know that he had been invited to the yacht club. Paul seemed interested that his parents had made the gesture, but not, so far as Lawrence could tell, either pleased or displeased about it.

"They do that," Paul had said. "They did that with my sisters' teachers, too. They really like to haul everybody in together. Are you going to go?"

"I thought I would," Lawrence said. "What do you think?"

"I don't know. Whatever you feel like. You don't have to worry about not going. It'll probably be huge. Drinks and lots of fancy eats. Terrific entertainment, too."

"That doesn't sound too bad."

"There'll be some advertising people there, and they're all right," Paul continued. "And there'll be some of my mother's book people, and . . . maybe some friends from school."

"What's the entertainment?"

"I'm the entertainment," Paul said.

❦

The party at the North Shore Marina was rather like the event Lawrence had imagined from the details Paul had provided. He had expected an assemblage of prosperous men and women in early middle age, perhaps eighty or a hundred—enough to fill the tables of a discrete annex. He had expected confirmation of his theory that physically attractive people like the Berrisfords typically gather other attractive people around them. The guests, including a number of decidedly bohemian illustrators, seemed to mix easily with one another, perhaps veterans of previous Berrisford hospitality and one another's company.

After about an hour of standing conversation and drinks, Paul appeared. He wore a blue blazer over a striped rugby jersey—the same clothes he had worn that day to school—and Lawrence was struck by how easily he was taken into the "executive" crowd, and on how much warm attention was focused upon him.

"So you came," Paul said to Lawrence when he had made his way through groups of other guests.

"Yes. Are you really the featured attraction? When do you play?"

"I'm the only attraction, unpaid. I play after dinner."

"Well, I'll look forward to that."

"You've heard it all, Mr. Lawrence."

Shortly before they were summoned into the dining room, Elizabeth Berrisford disengaged herself from a group of her husband's associates. She wore a black dress, simple in its cut and unadorned. She was brighter of eye, more vividly rouged than he had remembered her.

"You are nice to join us here, Mr. Lawrence," she said to him. "You've been so generous in your attention to Paul. We hoped we might thank you and get to know you a little."

"That's awfully kind of you. And I understand there's a concert in the works."

"A concert—oh, Paul. Yes, he agreed to play. Sweet boy. Bill's friends and my friends are all great fans of his." She peered over Lawrence's head. "It's time for dinner at last. Come along and let's see where we've seated you."

As Lawrence followed Elizabeth Berrisford into the dining room, he wished, almost as a child might, that he could stay near his hostess, near her easy familiarity and striking good looks. As it happened, Lawrence was placed at a table with Bill Berrisford, a pair of Mrs. Berrisford's' bohemian friends, and several of Mr. Berrisford's livelier business colleagues.

"Table of honor," Elizabeth Berrisford said, patting his arm as she left him.

Bill Berrisford, his face flushed, was thoroughly conscious of being host. His talk, shared equally among his tablemates, was of boating mishaps, a commercial filming project in California, Chicago's Polish sausages (a mock review of his most favored outlets), and the plans under way to expand pedestrian access to the streets and plazas of the city's Loop during the noon hour.

Berrisford seemed to like talking about the city, about the orchestration of developments that would affect thousands of people. Lawrence found him infectious, and impossible not to like. He was a physically big man, Lawrence realized, inches taller and much broader than his son.

As the dinner wore on, Lawrence decided that Bill and Paul Berrisford were radically unrelated in type and style, although some of the son's animal energy might be present in his father's demeanor. Lawrence could not imagine that any further schooling or sheer passage of years would confer on Paul his father's particular kind of social ease: the quick anticipation of other people's interests and needs that marks the natural impresario. Berrisford might be President, Lawrence thought. He would certainly play a credible President in a movie.

Why, Lawrence wondered, did the presence of this expansive, agreeable man seem to diminish Paul? Paul was certainly distinctive enough in his own right, and in an unrelated, untamed way, arguably as handsome as either parent. Yet, he did not seem even slightly continuous with the kind of man his father was. Bill Berrisford was, among other things, well off. Lawrence wondered if Paul would ever be well off. Unlikely, Lawrence concluded, though he had no reason to think Paul might not inherit money.

Paul did have a decided "rich kid's" carelessness about possessions and about his clothes. Still, Lawrence could not imagine him polished to the veneer of, say, the non-bohemian guests in the dining room. Lawrence studied Bill Berrisford for a moment as he demonstrated a point expressively with both hands. It was a marvel, Lawrence thought. In contrast to his father, Paul was a primitive. *Paul is a primitive.*

Lawrence pushed himself back slightly from the table and considered. He considered the glass walls of the dining room, the lanterns flickering on the docks beyond, the waiters in their linen coats, the white, antiseptic light cast by the track lighting overhead, the freshly cut flowers in the centerpiece, the heavy silver, the faint phrases of orchestra music emanating from another room, the impression of parties forming and re-forming, swelling in concentric rings outward from the marina to the sparkling hotel towers beyond to, perhaps, a great, fantastic network of wealth and pleasure extending through every artery of the city.

That was what Bill Berrisford meant, Lawrence realized. He meant activity and progress. He generated a Future, the actual Future of this city. And that was the difference in Paul. Paul was impossible to place in an actual, practical future. "I hate time," Paul had told him more than once.

When the desserts were being brought in, there was some hubbub among the waiters as they erected a set of portable risers and a stand where Paul would play. Lawrence spotted Paul at a nearby table. He had turned his back to the guests, his ear to the body of the guitar as he tuned it. A portable microphone was brought in, tested, and rejected.

At a signal from Bill Berrisford, somebody flicked the

lights on and off, and he called for the company's attention. With a pleasing offhandedness, he announced that Paul would play, joking that he was glad some of them had requested this particular entertainer, and even gladder about his fee. The guests laughed and applauded appreciatively. Paul grinned in his father's direction, with a smile that was both reticent and willing.

Without any words of introduction, Paul picked out a rich, jangling progression of ragtime chords. He bent low over his guitar as if listening for something, and began to sing in a husky whisper:

You gotta see Mama every night
Or you don't see your mama at all.

Either because of the playfulness of the tune or because some of the guests had heard Paul sing it before, there were murmurs of approval as he began. Lawrence marveled again at what an assured and economical performer Paul was. His partly distracted look, Lawrence was sure, resulted from a close monitoring of the sounds he was producing. He was listening to himself, listening and answering. Though as complete in his introverted preoccupation as his father had been effusively gregarious, Paul, like his father, commanded close attention. His voice grew in volume, a husky, accusing moan from the back of his throat.

If you want my company
Don't you fifty-fifty me.

Even if the staff had not dimmed the track lighting except for the light over Paul's stool, he would have become the exclusive focus of the guests' attention. Paul played for half an hour, a mixed selection of folk tunes, pop tunes, and, surprising to Lawrence, a ragtime version of "Anything Goes."

"That's it," he said simply when he finished. He grinned uneasily through the applause. The guests wanted more. Paul looked to his father, and Berrisford shrugged. Paul played a muted "Grandfather's Clock," the effect of which was to quiet the room to a point near breathlessness. Once again, the company gave him a warm ovation.

When the lights came up in the dining room, Lawrence had the unsettling feeling of being shifted too rapidly from one world to another. The intimacy and concentrated quiet of Paul's performance, he felt, had been dissolved too abruptly. Nor did the company's conversation, despite the appearance of more drink, rise to its previous pitch.

As people began to take leave of the Berrisfords, Lawrence rose to thank his hosts. Elizabeth Berrisford clasped his hand and thanked him once more for coming. "I know it meant a lot to Paul." Bill Berrisford seemed oddly spent and vacant when Lawrence shook his hand.

Once aboard the Evanston bus, Lawrence sat back to sort out his impressions. There was Elizabeth Berrisford: her brightness of eye, a lingering desire for more of her. Then there was the clash of the "two evenings": the evening of drinks and Berrisford's table talk, and the evening of Paul's performance. Did the guests' obvious pleasure in Paul's playing, Lawrence wondered, reflect still more favorably on his father?

Ordinarily, a son's athletic or artistic gift might be thought to enhance the esteem in which a parent is held by others. But Lawrence doubted this was the case. It seemed more likely that Paul's performance somehow canceled out his father's heartiness. The feelings Paul evoked seemed not to require the North Shore Marina, which seemed to quietly reject them. *Did Bill Berrisford ever sense this?* Lawrence wondered.

❧

In the weeks that followed, Paul and Juliana's spirits brightened steadily, or so it seemed to Lawrence. Their visits to his office were alive again with jokes, accounts of their mutual out-of-school adventures (they were systematically discovering Chicago, they said, North Shore to South Side), confidential plans, and schemes.

When they came to see him alone, each seemed surprisingly in need of reassurance that he or she was worthy of the other. Paul said that Juliana knew and read so much that he sometimes felt she was baby-sitting him. Juliana worried out loud that Paul would find her too rarefied, too far off the normal, healthy track. "We Francks are not even a hundred percent American yet," she said.

Lawrence was also gratified that they came to see him with their triumphs and prizes. Juliana had been admitted early to Columbia, Oberlin, and Brandeis. She was ecstatic about each acceptance. "There's *nothing* better than acceptance," he told her. "I recommend acceptance for everybody."

One afternoon after school, Paul entered the office carrying his guitar case. Without speaking, he shut the door, opened the case, and propped a knee up on the captain's chair to support the guitar.

"Ready for this?" he said, and ran a finger far up the fingerboard, producing a metallic whine. Then he played and sang "Terraplane Blues" with what Lawrence thought an unimaginable richness of feeling.

"Well, Paul, you got all of it, didn't you?" Lawrence said when he had finished. "Perfect. Just *perfect*."

"I got it." Paul's grin of pleasure seemed to warm the room.

"Has Juliana heard that one?"

"She's heard it a thousand times."

༒

Although a decidedly generous man, Lawrence, like many bachelors, gave little thought to gifts, either to receiving them or to giving them. But his unexpected midwinter buoyancy moved him to a number of exceptional acts. One of them was to remove *The Swabian Lovers* from his office wall one Saturday and take it to a North Side camera store, which made photo duplicates of color prints. The reproduction was, to Lawrence, indistinguishable from his own print, and he took it to a framer in Evanston, ordering the closest facsimile to his own frame they could produce.

The print was ready on Valentine's Day, and Lawrence asked a student office guide to deliver an official memo and passes to Paul and Juliana. The memo said to report to Guidance for an urgent appointment. Paul arrived first. "What's up?" he asked. "Is everything okay?"

"Everything is fine," Lawrence said deliberately. "Please be seated until Miss Franck arrives."

Paul's grin burst through obvious efforts to hold it back. "Yes, sir."

Juliana hurried in, noted that Paul was seated on the two-seater, and looked expectantly at Lawrence.

"As you two young people are possibly aware," Lawrence began, pacing behind his desk, "it is Valentine's Day. And while you clearly have no affectionate token for me—not so much as a cheerful 'Good afternoon'—I have one for you. It's not an *expensive* gift, you understand, but it is a gift from the heart on this day of the heart. To you both."

Lawrence handed Paul the print, which was wrapped in brown paper and string. Paul pulled the paper away from the picture and gave *The Swabian Lovers* a long look. Juliana moved close behind him.

"No, not your picture," said Juliana. "Oh—it's another one," she corrected herself, looking up to the print on the office wall. "It's a new one for us!" she exclaimed.

"This is really fine, Mr. Lawrence. No one has ever given me a picture in my life."

"Given *us* a picture," corrected Juliana.

"That's right," said Paul. "How do we divide it?"

Only then did it occur to Lawrence that Paul and Juliana could not possess the gift simultaneously. He had not thought of them as separate people living in separate homes. *Extraordinary*, thought Lawrence.

"I think I'll have to get another one made," Lawrence said.

"Absolutely not! That would change the gift entirely. No, this is what we'll do," said Juliana. "Paul will have the picture for the first two weeks, I'll have it the next two weeks, and so on, until such time as we live in the same room or we are dead."

"Sounds fair to me," Paul said, looking at Lawrence.

CHAPTER *Five*

———————

The gift of *The Swabian Lovers* had the effect of confirming Paul and Juliana's intimacy. The token seemed to confer official, or at least adult, acknowledgment of their exclusive preoccupation with each other. Lawrence had, in effect, "legitimized" them.

For his part, Lawrence found Paul and Juliana's love continually revitalizing. Conscious of the new familiarity all three of them felt after the December visit to his apartment, Lawrence had at first taken care to sound a muted note of moderation and responsibility. As that posture began to feel increasingly unnatural and inauthentic to him, he gradually relinquished it. He knew there was no longer any core of "guidance" in his relationship to them. What, he sometimes wondered, *was* his role? Confidant? Confessor? Friend? *I am content,* Lawrence told himself, *to reflect and to confirm.*

The fact of the matter was that, increasingly, Paul and Juliana seemed right to him—at first emotionally, then ethically, and the counter forces of moderation seemed self-centered and weak. By early March, Lawrence began to see the dynamics of the high school differently. The throngs of students who flowed through the corridors during passing periods seemed lost and drifting, manipulated by routines they had neither designed nor agreed to and for reasons they had neither the head nor the heart to question.

Except for Paul and Juliana, each advisee he was assigned to see individually seemed dull, inarticulate, only half awake, only half alive. Because these students seemed so flat and unresponsive when he was with them, he did not feel any authoritarian twinge when helping to bump them along, out into the hall for the next period, the next grade level, college.

The administration and evaluation of standardized tests—Lawrence's chief responsibility—had become almost unendurably tedious to him. During a massive sitting of the SATs, a random image had popped into his head and refused to leave him: the tests—the whole complex of standardized tests to which students are subjected in schools—are a great grid of bird seed. Each tiny square of the grid contains densely packed kernels of the blandest, palest birdseed that can be produced. Periodically, students are crowded onto perches facing the grid and told to peck for all the seed they can get in the time allotted. Ready, get set, go. Peck, peck, peck . . . peck, peck, peck. The birds look foolish, irritably pecking at the grid from their crowded perches. The air in the cage grows gamy. Seeds are knocked loose from the grid and fall to the floor. Others are only half cracked and passed by.

Some birds—the nervous, beaky ones—get a kernel almost every peck. Others miss, peck between the kernels, and finish with nearly nothing. Afterward, the birds are shunted back to the main cage. Not one of them imagines a lawn, a pond, a forest, or a jungle. But if into the cage of little gray birds there is placed an oriole, outsized and brilliant, and if the oriole, turned the wrong way on the perch, catches the bright black eyes of an indigo bunting idle on a distant perch. . .

"Mail," announced Betts Storey, dropping a bundle of bag-brown Educational Testing Service envelopes, and a smaller white one, onto his blotter.

Lawrence picked up the personal letter. His name and address were inscribed beautifully in a kind of practiced calligraphy he could not identify. The return address indicated it was from the Francks.

11 March

Dear Mr. Lawrence,

My husband and I did not want to let the school year pass without declaring our gratitude and appreciation for the guidance and friendship you have given our daughter Juliana.

Your ears would burn if they could hear the praises she sings of you at home. Parents count themselves lucky if their children are given a few competent and inspiring teachers, but when someone at school takes a special, personal interest, that is an unexpected blessing.

Thanks also in part to you, Juliana is deciding among three very fine colleges and universities. There is something unique in each of them for her, and I know she values your opinion on such matters.

We could not be happier with her or more grateful to you. While we have not yet met you personally, Mr. Franck and I hope to arrange for that pleasure before Juliana leaves school.

Again we are grateful.

Sincerely,
Rachel Franck

Lawrence dropped the newly arrived testing materials onto the floor behind his chair. He read through Rachel Franck's letter again, then began to write her in reply.

❧

A March day on the rim of Lake Michigan will occasionally warm and thaw to the extent that winter's end can be imagined, but by nightfall the raw cold regains its authority. On such nights, Lawrence found his nocturnal walks especially bracing. This particular evening, something was stirring within him and, for all he knew, in the very heart of Evanston.

Even as a boy, Lawrence had been a solitary walker. Sometimes it seemed to him that only at his pace did information build itself into understanding. The town he had lived in as a boy, the college portals and walkways of New Haven, Chicago's lakefront, and now Evanston—walking somehow printed these settled neighborhoods like circuitry into his consciousness.

It was midnight when Lawrence, exhilarated, strode out the carriage house drive and down the street. Tonight would be a long one: past the Orrington Hotel, down along the university, along Sheridan Road, perhaps as far as the Berrisfords' house, up sharply to the stadium, then a gradual loop back home. It was cold, Lawrence reflected, wonderfully cold. He felt the usual, irrational pleasure of approaching the turnoff to Juliana's street, and when he did turn in the direction of the Francks' house, he stopped short at the sight of the one parked car on the street.

Not a driver himself, Lawrence was normally oblivious to the makes and styles of automobiles, but the Volkswagen parked beneath the streetlamp seemed familiar and significant. It was Paul's car. He was certain it was Paul's car. Lawrence moved across the lawn to the curb, noted the sunroof (did Paul's car have a sunroof?), and peered inside.

Wedged into the backseat floor space was the familiar guitar case. Odd for Paul to be at Juliana's after midnight on a Tuesday. Could there be some major test or paper? That didn't sound like Paul, nor would such a late-night study session conform to the strict policies Juliana had described as being in place in her household. And why was Paul parked nearly a block away?

Lawrence continued toward the Francks' house, situated in a void of darkness between streetlights. It was a large, settled, frame house with bowed bays on each side of a center entry. As Lawrence approached, he scanned the facade from the third-floor gables to the ground to see if lighted rooms suggested Paul and Juliana's whereabouts.

The house was entirely dark. As Lawrence passed, he cast a final searching glance along the side of the house and thought he saw something. A pale form seemed to pass across the narrow corridor of darkness between the Franck garage and the steps leading up to the back porch. Lawrence moved a few steps in from the walk and stopped still at the side of the driveway hedge. There was a faint metallic rattle from the darkness beyond the back porch, another glimpse of a shadowy figure. Someone in light trousers was moving across the Francks' back lawn. Could it be Paul?

Lawrence edged quietly behind the leafless hedge lining the drive. He stepped soundlessly along the wall of the garage, then peered around the corner. Not more than fifteen yards to his right stood the motionless figure of Paul (Lawrence was sure), holding a section of ladder at his side. Another section of ladder lay on the darkened lawn between Paul and where Lawrence stood. Lunatic boy! Lawrence wanted to laugh.

Paul stood still, looking up at the back of the house, probably, Lawrence guessed, waiting to see if the noise he made with the ladder had been heard inside. Lawrence thought about his own escape route if the lights suddenly went on inside the Franck house. Feeling uneasy, he imagined a patrol car pulling quietly up to the front curb to investigate. The trespass would be hard to explain, he mused, but not impossible.

Paul was now in motion again. He proceeded to the rear of a single-story extension protruding from the back of the house. The extension looked as though it might be an enclosed summer porch or a sunroom. It was supported by thick clapboarded columns at intervals of about six feet. A wooden railing enclosed the flat roof space above.

Paul held the ladder vertically and began to incline it slowly toward the house until it rested against the railing of the porch roof. Again the boy paused at the base of the ladder, staring up toward the darkened windows of the house. After a minute or two, he began, one deliberate rung at a time, to move up the ladder.

Paul could be shot, Lawrence told himself as he suddenly

felt an urge to catch Paul's attention, to advise him to abort his plan. He also felt an inexplicable sense of being in collusion with the boy, and, yes, even a feeling of superiority, of pleasure, in monitoring Paul's movements.

As Paul reached the level of the porch roof and placed a foot tentatively on the surface, Lawrence moved across the yard to the base of the ladder, watching his footing carefully in the darkness to avoid stepping on something that would make a noise. When he reached the ladder and looked up, Paul had disappeared over the railing.

A very loud scraping of wood on wood, of doors being forced open, caused Lawrence's heart to leap. Involuntarily, he pressed himself in close against the porch screening, held his breath, and waited. He peered through the screen to see if there was an open passage to the street on the other side of the house.

Lawrence heard an unintelligible, breathy exchange overhead: "You . . . said you really . . . right . . . now . . . can't believe you . . ." Then there were shushing sounds, silence, and giggles. It was Juliana. She had come out onto the rooftop. Lawrence heard the crackle of their footsteps as they approached above him. He forced himself farther into the screening, deeper into shadow.

"So this is your ladder," Juliana whispered. She sounded very near in the darkness overhead.

"It's actually your ladder." Giggles.

"I don't believe you did this."

"Hey, didn't I say I was coming? Didn't I say about one o'clock? Isn't it one o'clock? And if you didn't believe I was coming, why are you up, Miss Jewel?"

As Paul's voice passed from whisper into ordinary speech, Juliana again shushed him. There was a silence.

"I am up, Lord Berrisford, because I knew you'd come," she whispered.

Giggles.

"Let's sit down here," Paul whispered. "Here, put some of this around your shoulders. Nice night, eh?"

"I don't think I've ever felt colder all the way through in my life."

"Should I make a fire?"

More giggles.

"Is that better?" Paul's whisper was huskier.

"Of course it's better."

"But are you warmer?"

There was a silence.

"This is nice," said Juliana.

"That's because it's night. Night is what we need."

"I kind of like day, too."

"You know the only thing I like about day? Honestly? I like the three or four times I bump into you. The short times are as good as the long times. I get up and go to school in the morning and it's all a fog until the end of second period, when I leave Kaminsky's trig class, go from 226 to 242, go down the stairs, and halfway, on the landing turn, there you are. That's the first bit of day for me. Then there's the time when I'm leaving the cafeteria and you're coming in, and we talk."

"And you always stay past your bell."

"Your fault. And then there's sixth-period Guidance. And then there's after school till dinner. That's the day."

"It's a lot, isn't it?"

"No, it isn't a lot. It's no time at all."

"You're right," said Juliana. "It never feels like enough time. It's always about to be over. But I love it."

"I love you."

"Oh, do you? Please do. Please never stop."

Muted sounds, like purring.

"You're all I want, Paul. You're absolutely, completely enough."

"You've got me. I'm here."

A muffled sound, and more silence.

"What are we doing next?" said Paul.

"This."

"No, really. After the summer? Next year?"

"This. We'll do this."

"Am I going to follow you to college? Am I going to live in

your locker?"

"They don't have lockers in college."

"I'll live in your closet. I'll live in your desk drawer. I'll live in your purse."

"You won't fit."

"I'll fit. I can fit easily into your purse. Jewel, don't you know I can do anything?"

"I do. I know you can."

"As long as it's night."

Silence.

"I love you, Paul. I love you with all my heart and all my body and all my mind."

"That's all there is."

"Paul."

"*You.*"

Silence.

"So what's next?"

"Paul."

"I keep thinking about it. You can't go away."

"How could I ever go away from you? It's not possible. Don't even think about it."

"You sound like me."

"Good. I like sounding like you. In fact, I'd like to *be* you."

"Then you wouldn't be you, and where would I be?"

"You could be me."

"Then we'd be back where we were."

"Which is heaven. Which is perfect."

"I love you, Juliana."

"I love you, Paul."

Silence.

"We're the only two people in this city who have what they want most. The only two people who don't need anything."

"We're the only two people," said Juliana.

"If we died right now, it wouldn't matter, would it?"

"Actual dying? Not being anymore? I don't believe in dying. I really don't."

"Don't ever die, Jewel."

"I won't. I can't. You can't, either."

"Promise."

"Promise."

Silence.

"Oh, Paul, it isn't fair to be so happy."

Lawrence was startled to see a light go on inside the house. He could see a woman in nightclothes start to descend the stairs. With painfully stiffened knees, he edged along the screening around to the far side of the porch. *Let there be an opening to the street,* Lawrence pleaded to himself. There was. As Lawrence bolted, he could hear the scrape of the French doors to the roof being pounded open from within.

"What in hell is going on here?" a man's voice called out

angrily. "Rachel, call the police! Don't move, any of you. I have a rifle here—"

"Papa," Lawrence heard Juliana protest as he reached the walk and turned sharply away from the house. "Papa!" Juliana said again. "Papa, it's nothing."

"Stop, you!" Mr. Franck's voice rang over the rooftops, over Lawrence's ducked head. Lawrence heard the clank of the metal ladder striking concrete. "Stop, you! I see you! Rachel, call the police!"

"Oh, Papa . . ."

Lawrence passed Paul's parked car and turned the corner toward his house, relieved to put distance and darkness between himself and the Francks' home. Behind him he could hear the flapping of Paul's rubber soles moving over pavement, the slam of his car door, and the whine of his car's starter.

Lawrence thought he could hear Paul's car for blocks, stopping and starting, shifting and accelerating through the Evanston streets. By the time Lawrence reached the carriage house drive, all was dark and quiet.

❧

Lawrence rose from his desk and gestured to Paul to come in. "Well, Paul. Fancy seeing you second period. Have you been expelled?"

"I wish I was. What do you have to do to get expelled?" Paul flopped down on the two-seater.

"Hmm, it's not easy these days. But I suppose if you keep cutting second period, we could set the machinery in motion. You look tired."

Paul met Lawrence's gaze for the first time. "You look tired, too, Mr. Lawrence."

"I *am* tired," said Lawrence briskly. "I roam the streets late at night. What's your excuse?"

"Ready for this?" Paul began. "I think I really screwed up last night. Have you heard about it? Have you talked to Juliana yet?"

"No, I haven't. Not today."

"She's probably not here yet. If her parents ever let her come back."

"What happened?"

"Well, I screwed up. I screwed up for both of us." Paul looked away morosely. "Yesterday at around dinner time, coming back from the library, I dropped Juliana off, and it seemed . . . it just seemed like I was always dropping her off. Getting a minute with her between classes, getting an hour or two with her after school, maybe a long evening on the weekends . . . it just seemed like it wasn't enough, and that wasn't right."

"Paul, that's more time than most married couples spend

together," said Lawrence.

"I don't want to be like most married couples. I want to be with Juliana. Every minute I spend with her, I feel completely there. That's what feels real. The rest is just killing time until I'm with her again. You probably think I'm exaggerating, but I really mean it."

"I believe you. How did you screw up?"

"Royally. I told Juliana I was coming over to her house late last night after her folks were in bed—that I was going to come down the chimney like Santa Claus and spend my first night with her ever."

"And did you do that?"

"Not quite. I went over there about one, and got a ladder from behind their garage. Then I climbed up on the roof over the porch. Juliana's room has doors that open onto the porch roof in the summer. The idea was to meet her out there."

"Out on the roof?"

"Yes. Out on the roof. In the dark. Don't you believe me?"

"Of course I believe you."

"Juliana's parents don't. My parents don't. Juliana saw me climb up, or heard me, and she met me out on the roof. So we just talked out there in the dark. Then, all of a sudden, out of nowhere, lights were going on, people were yelling, Mr. Franck sounded like he was going to shoot me. I've never heard him like that. He's normally quiet—and barely there. This time he went berserk."

"What did he say to you?"

"Nothing, really. He was just yelling, telling me not to move, the police were coming. I don't think he knew it was me at first. He must have thought I was a burglar or a rapist. So, I just hopped back on the ladder, which began to slide off the roof, and I jumped and ran. Juliana was up there in her blanket. It was a mess."

"Have you talked to them since?"

"No, I tried, but now they won't talk to me. When I got home, I could see I was in for it there, too. It was almost two o'clock, and the lights were all on downstairs. I just walked through the front door—straight into it."

"Straight into *what*?"

"Straight into ice. My mother met me in her bathrobe and made me sit down. She wouldn't even talk to me until my father got off the phone."

"Talking to the Francks?"

"Yep. I went into the kitchen and asked if I could talk to the Francks myself, but they wouldn't talk to me. They told my dad they didn't ever want to see me again. My father was into it, I'll tell you. I thought he might hang up the phone and hit me."

"Does he hit you?"

"He never has. Not yet."

"So he was really angry."

"Christ."

"So what have they done?"

"Everything. They told me I'm obviously too immature to have the freedom they've given me, so they said they're taking it all back. They're going to make all my decisions for me from now on."

"They're going to make the decisions."

"Yeah. I'm supposed to stay home at night now, even on weekends, until they tell me otherwise. The VW goes. Not just for a while—they're getting rid of it. And they're going to take me to look at boarding schools, which I'll have to transfer to unless my grades and all of my reports improve."

Paul thrust his legs forward so that he was almost reclining against the back of the two-seater. He crossed his arms up over his eyes. "And there's supposed to be no Juliana. We're obviously not a 'good influence' on each other."

"That sounds like the works."

"That's it. That's what they say. And they've got it all wrong, too. Mr. Franck thinks I went into Juliana's room, that that's what we were doing. At least that's what he told my dad, and that's what my parents, and I guess the Francks, think. They don't believe we were sitting and talking on the roof in the cold. But we were. That's just what we were doing."

"It's probably hard for them to imagine."

"Do you believe me—that we were just talking on the

roof?"

"I do, Paul," said Lawrence. "That sounds like you two."

The bell rang, signaling the passing period between class-es.

"What do you think, Paul? Have you recuperated enough to face third period?"

"Why not?" said Paul, still reclining, his arms covering his face.

Lawrence hastily inscribed a pass. "Give this to the Dean's secretary on the way to class. It may keep you from losing meal privileges at home."

Paul took the pass. "Thanks. Thanks a lot, Mr. Lawrence. You know something? I'm a goner."

"I think you're very tired."

"Yeah, I'm tired," said Paul on the way out. "*And* I'm a goner."

⁂

That afternoon, at a little past four-thirty, Lawrence switched off his office light and began locking the door behind him when he saw Juliana sitting in the waiting area in front of Betts Storey's desk.

"Juliana! Have you been here long? Why didn't you knock or come in?"

"You had people. Then I went out for a while. I just came back. Can we talk a minute?"

"Of course. Come in." Lawrence unlocked his door and motioned Juliana inside. Juliana looked startlingly unwell.

"You look as if you're having a bad time," Lawrence said gently. "Paul told me about last night."

"Paul doesn't know everything." Juliana's chin trembled, and she began, in a muffled way, to cry.

"What doesn't he know?"

"He doesn't know—" The dam burst and she sobbed out loud, bending forward at the waist so that her hair fell over her knees. Lawrence reached for a box of tissues from his bookshelves and placed it on the cushion next to her. "He doesn't know that I'm not supposed to see him anymore. Any more at all."

"I think his sentence is the same. But it sounds to me like the first thing worried parents might do when they're upset. It's hard to stay that upset. I'll bet things look brighter and more negotiable in a few days."

"Oh, Mr. Lawrence," Juliana began, pausing to wipe her eyes and nose, "you don't know my parents. They mean this. They're acting like they don't know me. They say they can't believe me anymore." Juliana sobbed convulsively. Lawrence felt his own throat begin to tighten. He felt he should hold her, draw her head to his chest and rock her gently back and forth until she stopped crying. *I would do that*, Lawrence told himself, *if she were my daughter or my niece.*

"Your parents love you, Juliana. Even if they don't understand last night, even if they've got things all wrong, it's because they love you and are worried about you. Believe me, they won't sustain their disapproval. Or too, they'll realize they're dealing with the old Juliana again, and this crisis on the roof will get put in perspective, and things will settle back to normal. Believe me, it happens every time."

Juliana was silent.

"You know what I'll bet?" Lawrence asked.

"What?"

"I'll bet before the year is out, the roof episode becomes one of the funniest jokes in the history of the Franck family."

"Mr. Lawrence," Juliana said, fighting for control, "they don't want me to see Paul out of school at all."

"Do you think they'll insist on that forever?"

"I think they'd like me not to see him again, ever."

"Propose something to them in a week or two, when everything looks less dire."

"Mr. Lawrence," Juliana said very quietly, "I love Paul."

"Yes, I know you do."

"I don't think you know the way I love him. I don't think he's cute. I don't have a crush on him. I love him. I love him from the inside out. He's the thing that feels most real in my life. Being with him is the reason for everything. I can't talk about it or explain it any better than that. He's all that matters. It's as if he's a gigantic, bright star out there drawing me into him, I'm whirling into him, and everything else is black."

Juliana's voice had gained strength. He had never heard her speak with such conviction.

"Last night," she continued, "if you could've heard Paul, if you could've heard what he was saying and how he was saying it, before my parents woke up, you'd know what I mean about him and why I feel this way. I don't think anybody really knows Paul but me. He's the sweetest, the kindest, the most open and honest person I've ever known, that I will ever know."

"You know the reason he worries his father? You know the reason he's a loner in this school—in spite of the fact that he's brilliant and talented beyond description, and beautiful? The reason is that he's so honest and natural that he threatens people. He does. My friends think he's gorgeous, but strange. Their boyfriends put him down behind his back. They'll say anything—that he's crazy, that he's a snob, that he's a hippie. They just can't take somebody who says only what he thinks and who won't say anything he doesn't think. Mr. Lawrence, Paul is so beautiful. He's such a miracle. I thank God every second that we wandered in here this fall.

"But he's out there by himself right now, Mr. Lawrence." Juliana was growing a little shrill. "He's out there by himself, and he could do anything. I mean, you don't know him. He has absolutely no protection, no protective coating. He can get hurt, he can get lost so easily. You don't know what I'm saying, do you?"

"I think I do, Juliana."

"It's that he's all right, he's himself with me, and he isn't any other way. I can't explain this."

"I think I see," said Lawrence. "Are you worried that Paul will do something impulsive, that he will hurt himself?"

"Yes. Yes, I'm worried. Because I know he'll do something impulsive. That's the only way he acts. But I don't think you see, I don't think anybody sees, that he's the one who's being hurt . . . Oh, my God."

"What?"

"My parents have been waiting outside for fifteen minutes. They're picking me up at school now. I'm late. I can't be left alone anymore." Juliana got up to go.

"Juliana, one thing," Lawrence said, rising with her. "I know you're upset and worried, and probably tired right now, but I want you to know that I'm glad you stopped in to tell me what you're feeling. I also want you to know that your guidance counselor believes you really love Paul and that Paul really loves you, and that it's not kid stuff. What you're feeling, Juliana, is wonderful. And it's true. It's truer than anything. Don't give it up. I know you won't."

"No, I won't. Thank you, Mr. Lawrence. I needed you."

CHAPTER *Six*

Nothing about the exterior of the Francks' house, a comfortably settled arrangement of bays and gables, prepared Lawrence for the beauty inside. The center hall was wainscoted to the ceiling with dark wood, and on either side, doors paneled with leaded glass opened onto elegant, spacious rooms. To the right, where dining furniture might have been expected, there was an arrangement of straight-backed chairs, music stands, and what Lawrence assumed to be the cases holding cellos and violins.

"The music room," Rachel Franck explained with a wave. "This is one of the few quiet times in the Franck household."

"I'm sorry that it is," said Lawrence, following her to the left through an agreeably formal living room of Oriental carpets and elaborately carved furniture. At the back of the living room, another set of glass doors opened to a wainscoted den with a large bowed bay of mullioned glass. Beyond that lay the back garden.

"Make yourself comfortable, please," said Rachel Franck, "while I fetch the tea things."

When Juliana's mother left the room, Lawrence rose from

his chair and moved to the bay window. When she returned, wheeling a teacart, he was looking distractedly in the direction of the balustraded summer porch.

"I think it's trying very hard to be spring, don't you?" she said.

After the tea had been poured, Rachel Franck said, "You're very kind to come so quickly. I know it cannot be easy to get away during school hours. But I think it's best to talk when it's quiet, when Juliana and the others are in school."

"I was glad to come."

"Mr. Lawrence, you know Juliana quite well, I think, and you also know the Berrisford boy. Juliana positively adores you and thinks of you as her ally against her cruel parents. Which is why I wanted this opportunity to explain how Julius, Juliana's father, and I feel about what has been happening to her.

"Juliana seems to us—and, of course, we are her parents— an exceptional girl, a girl with very deep feelings. She has always been quite grownup in many ways. She helps me with the others. She's so responsible with her schoolwork and with her music. She has given us no trouble, even when she was a baby. She has always been . . . such a dark, eager thing. And she has been very close to us, too. We are so grateful for that, because that does not always happen, as you know.

"But there is the other side to Juliana, too, which worries

us. She seems so bright and accomplished in her talk, even among our friends, that people forget sometimes that she is still very much a child. This is true, Mr. Lawrence. She has not had, like some of her friends, a series of young male friends in school. She has not bothered us to go to the parties, and she has not been anxious, we don't think, to drink and smoke and carry on until all hours.

"Which is why, I think, this Berrisford boy has had such an effect on her. It is as if . . . all of the energy and desire to discover a young man and her own feelings of womanhood were set free at once. And this boy who has attached himself to her has received the full force of her romantic feeling. Am I making sense to you?"

"Yes, complete sense. And I think you're right. She feels very strongly about Paul Berrisford, and he feels equally strongly about her."

"Yes," continued Rachel Franck, "but there is no proportion there, no moderation. I don't know where good judgment and restraint come from in such matters. But I do know that Juliana doesn't seem to have any at the present. There is only this boy, Paul. You know him well, Mr. Lawrence? What do you think of him?"

"Oh, I like him very much, Mrs. Franck. He's a little hard to describe, but some of the things you just said about Juliana apply to him, too. Outwardly, he seems very independent and in control, but inwardly he's very uncertain and vulnerable. He's a little less than a year younger than Juliana, but sometimes he seems like a little lost boy."

"Have you met his parents, the Berrisfords?"

"I have met them, but I don't really know them. They're both very attractive."

"Yes," said Rachel Franck, "and the boy is also attractive, but, poor thing, he looks to us so much like an orphan. This fall, when he first began coming around to our house, we all took to calling him 'Juliana's orphan boy.' It was our joke, until Juliana got angry with it. Such an unmade bed. You just want to scrub him, press his trousers, brush his hair. Listen to the mother speaking." Rachel Franck smiled warmly.

"He *is* a little disheveled," Lawrence agreed. "But he's a good boy."

"I suppose they all are when you know them," Rachel Franck continued. "But this has not been good for Juliana. We have seen her change before our eyes from an affectionate, high-spirited young woman to a withdrawn and irritable one. This will not do, Mr. Lawrence. Until now, Juliana would talk to us about anything and everything. She delighted in it. And now it's 'Yes,' 'No,' and 'That's fine,' and away she goes to her room."

"But you don't suppose that's permanent. Don't you think she's still hurting from the roof incident?"

Mrs. Franck looked lost.

"The night when Paul climbed up to your porch roof?"

"Yes," said Rachel Franck, as if steeling herself. "And that is another thing. I cannot know your opinions about these things in advance, Mr. Lawrence, but we are old-fashioned Viennese. We are not very modern in our views about sex. The parents of Juliana's school friends seem to feel that as soon as the child is physically able to experience sexual feelings, then it is the parents' duty to set them up with birth control and anything else that will make sex for their children convenient.

"This is not how our family sees it, Mr. Lawrence. If we are wrong about this, so be it. Our children can correct us in our old age. But I do not think we are wrong. I think there is abundant evidence in this city and in this country that we are not wrong. I feel strongly that sex is not for children, even when they are fully-grown like Juliana and nearing the end of their childhood. Sex and all of its intimacies are for people who are ready to live with each other for a lifetime and to bring children into the world. I am sorry, but that is our view."

"No need to be sorry," Lawrence said. "I think that may be my view, too, although, as a bachelor, I'm no expert on such matters. I have a question, though. That night when Paul met Juliana on the roof—do you and your husband think that was a sexual . . . adventure?"

"It was not an hour for ordinary socializing, and hardly the time or setting for conversation. Really, Mr. Lawrence, I am the last person in the world who wishes to think the worst of my daughter in this respect, or of the Berrisford boy for that matter, but when a young man takes a ladder to the walls of our house and visits our daughter in her bedroom, where she is wearing only her nightdress—now, really."

"The reason I ask," said Lawrence, "is that, having talked to them both about the incident. I don't think sex was the reason for the visit. For what it's worth, I also don't think Paul went into Juliana's room. I think they met each other on the roof and stayed there until you heard them."

"They told you this? Both of them?"

"Yes."

"And you believe it?"

"Yes."

Mrs. Franck looked weary. "Well, God bless you, Mr. Lawrence, for such faith in the innocence of the young. That was not, however, my husband's impression, and he was the one who actually found them. If Juliana was out in the cold, she was outside in only her nightdress." Mrs. Franck breathed a long sigh. "It is a little hard for me to accept that they were simply visiting up there in the middle of the night. They were allowed to visit freely anywhere in our house, except Juliana's bedroom, during waking hours. As far as we could tell, they visited together for hours on end every day. There was no need to sneak into the house in the middle of the night for more visiting. This is not our Juliana."

"Children are continually surprising, aren't they?" said Lawrence, hoping to close the interview on a vaguer, more optimistic note.

"Juliana thinks this is all a matter of life and death," continued Rachel Franck, ignoring Lawrence. "But it is just the kind of thing she will thank us for when she is . . . free of all this."

᠅

That day, Lawrence returned to his office to find his brass-mounted pen set moved to the center of his blotter. A note was impaled on one of the pens. The message was written in large, eccentric printing:

Dear Guidance Counselor,

You are needed urgently for a dangerous appointment. Two (more or less) of your guidees are in distress.

If you have the courage to accept this urgent call, make your way, somehow, to the spot marked on the map below by four o'clock p.m. today.

This mission is secret as well as urgent. If anyone finds out, two (more or less) of your guidees are doomed.

Search your heart.

Urgently and secretly,

Was this on the level, Lawrence wondered, a little irritated. How seriously, he thought, was he supposed to take "urgent" and "doomed"? The map was not fanciful, though. Arrows indicated a succession of Evanston streets leading from the high school to Sheridan Road, out to a spot in residential Wilmette, apparently right on the shore. The blobbed spot on the map was labeled *BEACH HOUSE (GRAY SHINGLES)*.

Lawrence was able to borrow Alix Devereaux's car with the understanding that they would meet at the Orrington Hotel at half past five for dinner. The slight sense of irritation Lawrence felt reading the childish note intensified somewhat during the afternoon.

Am I becoming the extension of an adolescent game? Am I enabling it, Lawrence wondered, drawing on a term he did not care for from the jargon of chemical dependency. *Have I let myself be suckered into this game because these two children are so physically beautiful and I am forty-one?*

Lawrence passed through the corporate limits of Evanston into Wilmette, slowed down, and scanned the signs for the turnoff to the lake. The paved lane, when he found it, became stone and dirt after a few hundred yards, and he slowed Alix's car as he nosed past emergent greenery on each side. A weathered sign at the terminus of a small gravel cul-de-sac said *BEACH HOUSE*. Lawrence parked the car and, on foot, followed a path through the brush. Ahead of him, he could hear the powerful scrape and drag of the lake breaking over the shore.

The path widened to reveal the side door of a shingled building, closely hugging a bend of limestone ledge, which fell away sharply to rocks and a thin strip of beach below. The lake, a metallic gray, mounded gigantically along the horizon. A few yards from the beach house door, a steep set of wooden steps, almost ladder-like in their verticality, led down to the strip of beach.

Lawrence heard Juliana's voice inside. "He's here."

The weathered door swung open, and Paul and Juliana met Lawrence on the steps.

"You found us," Paul said.

"The map was clear," said Lawrence.

Lawrence entered a long, narrow room scattered with worn, unpainted wicker furniture, sun-bleached cushions, and straw carpets. The lake side of the room was a sweeping wall of glass, interrupted every few feet by vertical posts. An adjacent wall was dominated by a craggy fireplace of gray stone. A fire had been lit, which to Lawrence contrasted incongruously with the brilliant panorama of lake and sky beyond the windows.

"Does this house belong to someone we know?" Lawrence asked. "Or are we trespassing?"

"It belongs to us," said Paul, looking dressed for the beach in a faded rugby jersey, baggy khakis, and boating moccasins. "To us and to my Uncle Mort, who lives across the highway."

"He knows you're here?"

"Right! Nobody knows we're here, or else we wouldn't be here. My uncle stays in Florida till summer, and my family never uses this place until it gets hot enough to swim. So we're safe."

"Safe, but I hope not sorry," said Lawrence, some of the afternoon's irritation audible in his voice. "This is an illicit meeting, right?"

"It's not illicit," Paul said.

"It's against the rules your parents have set down for seeing each other out of school, isn't it?"

Juliana looked drawn. Paul said, "I think it's more like civil disobedience. Putting a higher value before a lower one, and risking the consequences for doing it."

"It doesn't look as though you're risking very much, with

all this sneaking around and secrecy. That's not the way civil disobedience works. With civil disobedience, you announce your intentions openly, because you're proud of them and because they can stand the light of day. And you don't hide yourself from authority. You present yourself to it openly."

"We can't very well present ourselves openly to our parents, can we?" said Paul gloomily.

"You can, but there would be consequences."

"Like never being allowed to see each other again."

"What do you think the verdict is going to be if your parents find out you've been seeing each other on the sly?"

"We've already received the verdict," Paul said. "The verdict and the sentence. How could we be worse off?"

"I can think of ways. Look, I don't like the feeling of conspiring with you against your parents. And you know I think the world of you both."

"We don't want to conspire either," said Juliana. "But it's either conspire or lose each other."

"Those are just the alternatives in the short run. In the long run, I'd bank on your patience and your obedience winning out. By doing this, by acting against your parents' will and behind their backs, you're confirming their worst fears about you."

"I can't follow that," said Paul. "Or maybe I don't want to. I can't go with this short-term, long-term business. There's no difference to me. What's real is what you're doing now. That's very short-term. Very short-term is all there is, just one bit of it after another until you die."

"I'm sorry we put you in a bad position," Juliana broke in. "We didn't think. We just wanted to talk with you, outside of school. We thought it'd be easier."

"We also thought it'd be fun," said Paul, tossing a stick of kindling against the fire screen.

"What is it you wanted to talk about?" Lawrence asked. "What's up?"

"I think you might like this," Paul said. "It's slightly practical."

"It can't be," Lawrence said, and they laughed.

"The idea," said Juliana, brightening, "is that I don't go away to college next year."

"What would you do instead?" Lawrence asked.

"Lots of things," said Juliana. "I'd get a job. I'd have much more time to work on my cello. I could take some courses."

"And live at home?"

"If it works, and if everybody gets along. Otherwise, I could get an apartment on my own."

"Mm. And what about the beach boy here. How does he figure in your plans?"

Juliana smiled wonderfully. "The beach boy would be a senior. He'd be playing soccer, and playing the guitar, and seeing me."

"And that's going to be allowed? Have you sprung this idea on your parents yet?" Lawrence asked.

"No," said Juliana. "It's hard right now. Things are at an all-time gloomy low at the moment, although I'm no longer under house arrest. I'm going to wait a few days and ease up to it. I'm going to stress the music part of it and how much more practice and instruction and performance I could get if I stay home. The problem is that the colleges want a deposit by the fifteenth. That's just a week from today."

"What do you think?" said Paul. "A good plan?"

Lawrence hesitated. "Its strongest point, in my opinion, is that it *is* a plan. You've actually thought ahead. On that score, you're way ahead of last week. The positive outcome is that you and Paul don't have to separate. The negative side is that Juliana's education is suspended."

"No, no," said Juliana. "That would depend on me."

"You're right. I suppose it would. But, also, what's your strategy to convince your families to lift the ban on your seeing each other?"

"We're working on that. We're still thinking about that one," said Juliana.

"They'll get tired of the bother," said Paul, "we'll keep going underground, or we'll have flat-out civil disobedience like you said."

"I wasn't recommending it," Lawrence said. "I was clearing up the definition."

"Well, those are the alternatives, aren't they?" said Paul.

"They are, the way you see it," said Lawrence, who could not bring himself to name other alternatives. "But you're right, Juliana, there still are some issues to be resolved. I think your parents are awfully happy right now with the prospect of you going to Columbia or Oberlin or Brandeis."

Paul placed a chair cushion on the straw mat in front of the fire screen and reclined on the floor. "We could also run away together and disappear," he said.

"Where'd you go?" Lawrence asked.

"Toronto," said Paul decisively. "Toronto's the place. It's a great city. It's like somewhere in Europe, except it's simpler and cleaner. We'd get by there. We'd play and perform and give lessons and wait tables. It'd work fine."

Juliana looked down at Paul with what seemed like reverence.

"It'd be like 'The Scholar-Gypsy,'" Paul continued, his eyes closed. "Juliana would be the scholar, I'd be the gypsy."

"I think Juliana's plan might be more promising." Lawrence heard timidity and brittleness come into his voice.

"Or we could swim out to sea here and never be heard from again," Paul said, crossing his hands on his chest.

"This very sea?" Lawrence asked.

"This sea would do fine," Paul said.

"I think it'd be cold," Lawrence said, smiling at Juliana. She did not return his smile. Instead, she turned her sad gaze to Paul, lying as if asleep on the mat in front of the fire.

"You know," Lawrence began expansively, "the swimming-out-to-sea idea is greatly overrated, I think. Have you heard of Evelyn Waugh?"

"Afraid not," said Paul, his eyes still closed.

"*Brideshead*," Juliana said. "*The Loved One.*"

"That's the one. A very funny writer, and a very good one, too. When he was young and just out of college, he was feeling really low. He didn't know what to do with himself, so he got a job, a terrible job, teaching in an awful boarding school in Wales. He'd written a novel, and mailed it to his friends back at Oxford. They didn't think much of it and sent it back to him with a dismissive remark. That was enough for Waugh.

"One dreary evening, he made his way down to a desolate patch of shore, took off his clothes, and left them there with a note. He waded into the dark water and swam out into the Irish Sea. Not very far out, he was stung by a jellyfish, which irritated him so much he returned to shore, where he resumed his life."

"Good for him," said Juliana, after a pause.

"Wouldn't have that problem in Lake Michigan," said Paul.

"I suspect there'd be other problems . . . Hey!" exclaimed

Lawrence, looking at his watch. "I'm late. I'm rudely late. I was supposed to meet Miss Devereaux at the Orrington Hotel twenty minutes ago. And I have her car." Lawrence rose from his wicker chair. "I've hardly even had a look at this incredible view. My God."

"Mr. Lawrence," Paul said, rising also. "Do you have to say you saw us here?"

"I should," Lawrence said. "But I won't . . . if you two promise me you'll remember the first thing I told you when I came in."

"Which was?" Juliana asked. "We will."

"I told you that nothing good will come from sneaking around and deception, that what's really good can always stand the light of day. This is not civil disobedience. This is private disobedience. That's the Lawrence message. Treasure it in your hearts. Now I've got to go. Take care of yourselves, you two."

"We will."

"Thank you for coming, Mr. Lawrence."

After bolting for the door, Lawrence reached the car, turned it around, and headed cautiously toward the highway and his date with Miss Devereaux.

CHAPTER *Seven*

Julius and Rachel Franck rose from the two-seater. They looked, Lawrence thought, no less distressed than when they had entered his office an hour earlier.

"What hurts us most is the defiance," said Julius Franck, arranging his raincoat over his arm. "Without a word to either her mother or me, she wrote to each of the universities saying she would not be attending. What it took her all these years to earn, she canceled out with a single impulse."

"The doors are not all closed," said Lawrence. "I know this recent business has been upsetting, but girls as bright and as interested in learning as Juliana have a way of educating themselves in any circumstances."

"Well, let us hope so," said Julius Franck. "Let us hope so."

He touched his wife's arm as a signal to go, then paused to look at *The Swabian Lovers*. "Juliana has this picture in her room. I have seen it there, haven't I?" he asked his wife.

"She has had it in her room. It is gone now. I believe she shares it with the Berrisford boy."

Rachel Franck looked unhappily at Lawrence and left the office with her husband.

Lawrence felt badly for the Francks. He could plainly see how, from their standpoint, what had appeared to be a bright and unlimited future for Juliana now looked cloudy at best. The very source of their concern—Paul Berrisford—was still an active presence in her world, and every new gesture on their part to diminish his influence seemed only to increase it.

During their meeting, Juliana's father had likened Paul to a "drug" whose hold over his daughter could only be "broken" by complete abstinence, externally and forcefully imposed, if necessary. "Mr. Lawrence," he had said, "can you imagine what it is like to see a daughter transformed from a happy, vivacious girl to a sullen, secretive one in a matter of months? It is as if we are losing her before our very eyes."

It was the first of May, and Lawrence, despite a frenetically looping wasp, was glad he had opened his office window wide. He had forgotten such days were possible. Outside, the light was green-gold, yellow, and white, and above the waving branches, the sky was a vibrant blue. The light blanched the hair and skin on the window side of Juliana's face as she sat in the two-seater. The promise and languor of the bright midday seemed to Lawrence at war with the girl's trouble—trouble which seemed now to fill the room.

"What have you got there?" Lawrence asked, gesturing to the bundle of books at her side.

"This? It's Matthew Arnold's *Lyric and Elegiac Poems*. It's got 'The Scholar-Gypsy' and 'Thyrsis'."

"And are you liking them?"

"They're beautiful. I practically know them by heart."

Lawrence recited:

Come, let me read the oft-read tale again:
The story of the Oxford scholar poor . . .

Juliana met his eyes and continued:

Who, tired of knocking at Preferment's door,
One summer morn forsook
His friends, and went to learn the gypsy lore.

"Yes," said Lawrence, "you *have* been reading Arnold. Don't you find him, in a perfectly satisfying way, to be about as gloomy as you can get? He manages to be both gloomy and stirring."

"I think the poems are beautiful. I think there's only one gloomy thing about them—and it doesn't come from the poems. It comes from reality." Juliana looked at Lawrence sharply. "The thing I can't bear, the thing I can't stand to think about, is that all the scenes in the poems are gone. They don't exist any more. They can't be found anywhere on earth."

"Oh, I don't know," said Lawrence, moved by her seriousness. "I wouldn't decide that too quickly."

"Mr. Lawrence," said Juliana, sitting erect, "do you think there still are meadows, in England or anywhere, where

> . . . Air-swept lindens yield
> Their scent, and rustle down their perfumed showers
> Of bloom on the bent grass where I am laid,
> And bower me from the August sun with shade.

Or a place where there are

> Roses that down the alleys shine afar.
> And open, jasmine-muffled lattices.

You know there aren't."

"No, Juliana, I don't know that." Lawrence paused to reconsider her question.

"There aren't. I'm absolutely certain there aren't. I don't mean there aren't tiny patches that somebody has preserved, something big enough to make a commercial in, but it doesn't go on and on past where you can see, the way nature originally did. I'll bet you can't walk one full mile up the

Thames anywhere in England and not see a power station or a water tower or some sharp-edged metal-and-glass thing that cancels out everything else. Can you deny that? Have you been to England lately? Paul has. He says Oxford is like here, only more cramped."

"I haven't been to England in twenty years."

"Never mind England. What about here? Have you seen an unruined mile of the Chicago River? The Des Plaines River? The Mississippi River? If we drove down to the southern tip of Illinois, could you find one meadow full of wildflowers that wasn't near a gas station or a toll road with green signs? This is what I think. I think every beautiful thing in these poems was there and was true, and I think all the beautiful medieval and classical things in Shakespeare and Keats were true, but they're gone now. You can never find them again anywhere in the world."

Lawrence looked hard at Juliana. Her color had risen, and her eyes were very bright. "Juliana, I find it distractingly beautiful right outside this window. Look."

Juliana turned to look at the sun-dappled wash of green and yellow outside. "It's a pretty day," she said. "I see a bike rack, a line of parked cars, and a UPS truck. And I know perfectly well, and so do you, what there is across the school lawns and around the corner."

"Do you think poets and painters care what's just around

the corner when they're creating a scene?"

"I don't know. I didn't mean to start an argument."

"I'm not arguing," Lawrence said.

"Good," said Juliana. "I mean, I'm sorry. I've just been feeling so trapped and cut off from everything. I used to think of myself as an extra-sensible and normal person. My interests and tastes were not the same as everybody else's, but my idea of right and wrong, proper and improper, normal and abnormal, felt right in line with everybody else's. But now I feel like a Martian or something. Things that are so obviously right and beautiful to me are horrifying to my family and everybody else.

"Paul, for instance—is there something wrong with him, Mr. Lawrence? Isn't he beautiful and funny and talented and sweet? Do you know a dangerous or mean side to him? How can the way I feel, which is the most complete and alive feeling I've ever known, be a mistake? Be bad for me? I just can't believe it. I can't accept that. Maybe I'm just odder than I thought, but what I'm feeling is true."

Tears began to move down Juliana's cheeks. "It's true, Mr. Lawrence, and if they take Paul away from me, then that great thing will be gone, just like the great things in these poems."

Lawrence struggled to think of something to say as Juliana bowed forward and wept. All he managed to do was to locate the box of tissues on the bookshelves and place it next to her on the two-seater.

ॐ

Tired from the past night's walk around the city's perime-
ter, Lawrence unlocked his office door. He also realized, with
vague satisfaction, that he had no clear obligation until mid-
afternoon. Without turning on the office lights, he sat down in
his swivel chair, stretched his legs out straight before him, and
reclined his head.

"Telephone for you, Mr. Lawrence," Betts Storey said over
the intercom. "Should I tell him you're in?"

No one calls at eight in the morning, Lawrence thought.
"Who is it? Do you know?"

"It's William Berrisford. Line one."

"I'm in."

Berrisford's greeting revealed once again a man daunting-
ly charged with energy.

"Mr. Lawrence, Bill Berrisford. I'd like to talk with you for
a minute, if I could, or maybe we should come in. It's about
Paul's SAT scores. Have you seen them?"

The College Board packet containing printouts of the junior class's scores lay unopened on the floor behind Lawrence's
chair. He could not remember exactly when they had arrived.
He guessed about a week earlier.

"No, I haven't seen them," said Lawrence. "Sometimes there's a delay."

"Well, Paul's are very interesting," said Berrisford. Lawrence felt his stomach contract unpleasantly in anticipation. "He got a 270 on the verbal section and a 300 on the math. That puts him, according to the booklet they sent along, in the bottom five percent of all those taking the tests this year. The bottom five percent in the nation. He's really outdone himself, hasn't he?"

"Have you talked to Paul about this?" Lawrence asked.

"We showed the scores to him last night. He just shrugged them off. He said he wasn't a test-taker. Which is just how he's been lately. Impossible. What do you make of scores like that? I didn't think scores went into the two hundreds."

"It's technically possible," said Lawrence. "He had to have done it intentionally."

"Well, we have to hope so," said Berrisford. "He can take them again, can't he?"

"As many times as he likes."

"That would be none," said Berrisford. "Goddamn that boy. He's just too cool a customer for his own good."

"He seems mixed up about a lot of things right now," Lawrence said, wishing that Berrisford would end the conversation so he could ruminate in the dark by himself.

"Well, it's time—maybe it's past time—for making things

clear and easy for him. His mother and I are scheduling a boarding school trip up through New England as soon as we can make the appointments."

"Mr. Berrisford, I don't have strong feelings for or against boarding schools generally, but the fact of the matter is that if Paul can subvert the SAT test, he can subvert his admission to boarding school. Also, good boarding schools only like to take willing customers."

"I know they do. We've thought about that. But the most important outcome from all of this business is for Paul to real-ize he's not calling the shots anymore. If he wants to, he can screw up this boarding school trip and all the interviews, but if he does, he loses his choice altogether, because then he's going to a place I pick out for him."

"Which is where?"

"Whatever I can find. Maybe even a military school. Don't worry, I'll find something."

"You're absolutely convinced about a boarding school."

"Yes, and frankly, it's the last thing we really want to do, all other things being equal. But we don't have a lot of options, do we? He seems to be going straight to smash. His SAT scores don't add up to six hundred. He does no work at home that we can see. He's becoming a lump. He's lost in space."

"I think he's still reacting to the ban on seeing Juliana," said Lawrence.

"Well, that may be," Berrisford said, becoming heated, "but what were our alternatives? If we'd let him go his way, he'd have married her already. As it was, he was climbing ladders into her bedroom in the middle of the night." There was a silence. "Are you still there? Hello?"

"I don't think that's quite right," said Lawrence. "It may not be the main issue, but I believe Paul just met her on the porch roof as a kind of lark."

"That's not what her father told me."

"He may be mistaken, too."

"I beg your pardon, Mr. Lawrence, but the man was there. He broke the thing up. You weren't there."

"As I said," Lawrence continued, "exactly where they met is probably not the point. I also don't want to sound unsympathetic to your concerns about Paul. I don't know what the answer is from a parental standpoint. Paul is in love with a girl who's in love with him. He can't see an open, honorable way to express his love, and he can't see how to proceed without it. That's his dilemma, as I understand it."

"Yes. It's a problem that's not going to solve itself, is it? Mr. Lawrence, thanks for your time."

ॐ

Lawrence felt awake and fully revived when Paul stopped

by his office during his free period after lunch.

"Hi, Paul," Lawrence greeted him. "I'm glad you stopped by."

Paul took his usual spot on the two-seater.

"Your father telephoned me this morning. About your SATs."

"What did he want you to do, change them?"

"No, I think he wants you to change them."

"I'll keep plugging away."

"Paul," said Lawrence. "Seriously, what did you do on that exam? Those are probably the worst scores ever registered at this school."

Paul looked up intently at Lawrence, who half expected an angry response. The line of Paul's lip began to waver, and unable to control his expression any longer, he burst into laughter. Caught off guard, Lawrence was unable to keep from laughing himself.

"Paul," began Lawrence, trying to regain composure, "Paul, what did you do?"

Giggling helplessly, Paul fell over sideways on the two-seater. Lawrence, after a few attempts to form a question, reclined his head over the back of the chair and waited.

Betts Storey appeared in the doorway. "What on earth?"

"This," said Lawrence flatly, "is guidance."

Paul quieted, relapsed into hilarity, then quieted again. "I filled in the answer sheet . . . diagonally. Do you know what I mean?"

"*Diagonally?*"

"Yes. I answered the first question A, the second one B, the third C, the fourth D, all down the test."

"You did that, instead of leaving the test blank?"

"Yes sir," said Paul.

"It's a much better system. My math score went way up."

"Yes, to 300."

"I'm not saying I'm going to rest on that score, Mr. Lawrence. I don't want to get cocky. But really, it's my verbal I'm worried about now. I'm not at all pleased with the 270. I think I can do better than that. Diagonals may not be the best approach there."

"Paul, your father's fed up. He says he's going to take you out of Evanston and enroll you in a boarding school."

"I know."

"You know. What're you going to do about it?"

"What I'm told."

"Paul, I'm serious. Your parents are making appointments to look at New England schools, and your father says that if you sabotage the process, he's going to get you placed in a school of his choice. He's talking about a military school."

"A military school?"

"Yes, if you sabotage the others."

"A military school."

"It's the kind of idea a father gets when his son makes diagonal patterns on his College Board examinations."

"You know, I regret the diagonals now." Paul grinned up at him with a brightness Lawrence had not seen since winter. "I had more of a zigzag pattern in mind"—Paul slashed the air with his forefinger—"but when I started to feel the old pressure, I fell back on the diagonals."

"Paul."

"What?"

"What're you going to do? Really?"

"What I said. I'm going to behave. I'm going to go along with my mum and dad to visit schools in New England. I'm going to be pleasant. I'm going to enjoy my parents' company, and I'm going to enjoy the scenery. I really like New England."

"Paul, are you being serious?"

"Completely."

"What about Juliana?"

"What about her? I love her."

"Are you prepared to be apart from her for a year or two?"

"No. Why?"

"Okay, let's start again. How does being agreeable and going off to boarding school allow you to stay with Juliana?"

"I'm not going to boarding school, and I'm not giving up Juliana, ever."

"Help me, then. I'm lost."

"I'm not going to boarding school. But I am going to be agreeable. I'm not only going to be agreeable, I'm going to be perfect. For three weeks."

"Because in three weeks your parents will soften and change their minds?"

"Because in three weeks my parents will be in Bermuda!" Paul flashed an anarchic smile.

"And you'll be home? Alone?"

"No, I'll be with my sister Sally."

"And she knows how to keep you in line."

"Sally? Sally can do anything. Sally loves me."

"What happens after Bermuda?"

"What happens?"

"About boarding school, about your parents, about Juliana? You know Juliana's already changed her plans for next year in order to stay here."

"After Bermuda will take care of itself."

"But it won't, Paul. Where has that approach gotten you so far?"

Paul was silent. When he rose to leave, his cheeks reddened. "If there's no after Bermuda, there's no after Bermuda." He turned towards the door.

"Paul, tell me one more thing," Lawrence said.

"Sure. What?"

"This morning, when your father and I were talking, I told

him I thought you were still reacting to the restrictions against seeing Juliana. He said that may be so, but what else could he do, that if you were given free rein again, you'd go off and marry her."

"*And?*"

"Is that what you'd do? What you wish you could do?"

"We *are* married."

Lawrence froze. His mind raced. It wasn't technically possible, legally possible.

"You are?"

"Maybe. It depends if there's a God," said Paul.

"I'm lost again."

"If there's a God—Juliana's certain there is—then we're married forever before Him. We've seen to that. If there isn't a God, then there's no marriage anyway, and we're just as married as anyone else."

"I'm going to have to think about that for a while, I guess."

Again Paul turned to go.

"Paul," Lawrence called after him.

"Mm."

"Can I help at all? Is there anything I can do?"

"Thanks, Mr. Lawrence, but I'm fine."

CHAPTER EIGHT

"Mr. Lawrence, I am so sorry to disturb you at home." Rachel Franck's voice, with its dulled German *r's*, sounded weary over the telephone. "But we have still another difficulty with Juliana. She tells us now she does not want to participate in graduation exercises. Someone there has told her that the diploma certificates can simply be picked up or mailed. Is that true?"

"I don't really know, Mrs. Franck, but I can check. Now that I think of it, I doubt that students are required to attend the graduation ceremony itself. But, of course, most students want to." Lawrence recalled endless successions of capped and gowned seniors inching their way toward the flower-bedecked gymnasium stage, always, it seemed, in airless heat.

"This is part of Juliana's anger at us, I am sure," said Mrs. Franck. "She says the ceremony is meaningless to her, but we know it is a way to hurt her father and me. We have invited family and friends from all over the city. It was to have been a happy celebration, with Juliana's favorite music. All the people who love her."

Certainly not all, Lawrence thought. "I don't know what to tell you, Mrs. Franck. This is a hard time, isn't it?"

"It should be such a joyful time," said Rachel Franck. "But Juliana insists on being miserable. And this has been going on for so long now."

Lawrence said nothing.

"Could you talk to her, Mr. Lawrence? I know this is not your responsibility. But Julius and I do not really feel we can say any more to her on the subject at home. We just feel that if she could end her schooling here on a more positive note, then maybe that would put all this recent unhappiness in perspective. She could start the next phase of her life in a . . . more productive way. But if we go along with her and let everything fall flat, this I know will add to her unhappiness. She is a girl seeking to be miserable, Mr. Lawrence."

"I feel for her," said Lawrence, "and for you. I'll be glad to talk to Juliana about attending commencement, and I wish I could guarantee she'll change her mind. But I can't."

"I know you can't. But I thank you very much for trying. You have been very kind to us."

"I couldn't bear it. I would suffocate," said Juliana, her eyes flashing with feeling. "I could probably get through the school part by acting like a zombie, but the idea of going home to a houseful of smiling relatives, opening a thousand gifts, and trying to smile and chat with my three thousand aunts—I can't do that. I won't do that. I know this is awful for my parents and that I'm being awful, but I don't have anything inside for that kind of thing right now. It's as though I've had some kind of surgery. Something's missing."

"What's missing?" Lawrence asked.

"You know what's missing."

"Paul."

"Yes, Paul."

"Well, he won't be missing for long," Lawrence said. "Aren't he and his parents due back from their New England trip at the end of the week?"

"I think so. But he'll still be missing for almost another week."

"Do you mean until his parents go off to Bermuda?"

Juliana said nothing.

"Juliana, have you made plans to rendezvous with Paul when his parents are away?"

"Heavens, Mr. Lawrence, does that sound like me?"

"Mm. Have you heard anything from him in New England?"

"It's not allowed."

"But have you heard from him?"

Juliana looked up at Lawrence and smiled faintly.

"Well, I have," said Lawrence. "He sent me a postcard.

Want to see?"

"Yes."

Lawrence handed Juliana a card tucked into the corner of his blotter. It depicted a harbor view of the New York City skyline at night. The high gloss finish of the card seemed to accentuate the gaudy sprinkle of white, yellow, and pink lights, like neon stars, among the huddle of dark buildings. The panorama included the Statue of Liberty, ghoulishly illuminated in copper green. On the reverse side of the card, Paul had written only, "This is Deerfield Academy."

Juliana's laughter seemed to take her by surprise. With her eyes crinkled at the corners and her mouth widened to its lovely smile, Juliana reminded Lawrence of her very first visit to his office, when she came to talk about college. He had never seen anyone of any age whose beauty so openly invited appreciation, he realized. *Do I love this girl*, Lawrence wondered without reflection, *or do I love her love?*

"Oh, where is he?" Juliana burst out, her eyes full of gladness.

❧

At the end of the week, a few minutes after the bell concluded the day's final class, Paul poked his head inside the door to Lawrence's office.

"Well, if it isn't young Berrisford," Lawrence greeted him.

"How's everything in the land of our ancestors?"

"Terrific," said Paul flatly. "Hi."

"Hi. Do you have a minute?" Lawrence gestured for Paul to be seated. "How were the schools?"

"They were all the same, but they were kind of interesting, too. The people all think you're dying to go there."

"Some of the candidates probably are."

"Yeah, I guess they are."

"How did the interviews go? Did you behave yourself? Did they give you any encouragement?"

"Actually, they did. Two of the admissions women who interviewed me had heard of my mother. They liked that I read books."

"It's a rare and impressive thing. So you really behaved?"

"I was perfect."

"Did you get along with your folks?"

"Perfectly."

"So what happens now?"

"Now I catch up on the work I missed, get ready for exams, brush my hair, and clean up my room."

"And then what?"

"And then my parents go to Bermuda."

"Yes, but I suspect they'll come back."

"They always have."

"So you're just going to take things as they come."

"How else can you take them?"

"The new, unflappable Berrisford. Have you seen Juliana?"

"Barely, for about two minutes. I really just got back."

"How do you think she is?"

"She's perfect."

At eleven the next morning, a Saturday, Rachel Franck called Lawrence at home to ask if he could come to their house for a Sunday afternoon of music, followed by a meal. She also thanked him for having taken the time to talk to Juliana.

Juliana, her mother recounted ecstatically, had agreed to go ahead with the commencement party they had planned and would, of course, attend the exercises as well. "She has really been a darling about it," she said to Lawrence. "I think we are getting her back. Praise God."

Lawrence wondered whether Juliana's decision might be part of a joint ruse to lower the parental guard. The school's graduation was a week after the Berrisfords would return from Bermuda. Perhaps Juliana was feeling more accommodating, more cheerful. If it was a ruse, Lawrence thought, it was a remarkably sustained and effective one.

Bill Berrisford called Lawrence the following Monday to ask that Paul's transcripts be sent to Deerfield, Pomfret, and Kent. "We've probably missed the very top of the line," Berrisford said, "but at least some of them are willing to look at him."

Berrisford also confirmed that Paul had behaved himself appropriately on the trip. "I think he's basically resigned to the fact. I also think the looniness and mooning around are over. At least, I hope they are." Like Rachel Franck, Berrisford thanked Lawrence warmly for his concern for Paul and for his help.

Hedgerow and treetop were decidedly green now, and the afternoon sky overhead was powdery blue, broken by bulbous formations of cumulus. Church spires, gables, chimneys, even the great elms, seemed heavy and ancient. As he made his way briskly toward the Francks' home, Lawrence wished that Evanston would retain forever this air of late afternoon.

As he turned up the walk, he heard the treble of the violins. On the front step, he hesitated, not wanting to interrupt the playing by ringing a bell. Then the door opened and Rachel Franck, smiling warmly and dressed in a long dress of wine-colored corduroy, beckoned him wordlessly into the front hall. Lawrence was surprised at the number of people inside, and that they were people of all ages.

To one side of the paneled entranceway, dozens of people, predominantly older women and young children, were seated about occasional tables bearing food and drink. To his right, in the music room, perhaps twenty or more adults were clustered about the musicians—at the moment, a trio playing beneath the chandelier in the center of the room. To Lawrence's ear, the playing was very good. It was something busy and crisp— Bach or Vivaldi.

On the far side of the musicians from Lawrence, Juliana stood beside her cello, attentive to the playing. She wore a simple, long-sleeved white blouse cut high on her neck, a long black skirt, and—striking to Lawrence—a hair-band of bright red velvet. She stood there with her beautifully burnished instrument before the sedately dressed company. The polished sideboard, the damask-covered walls, the Oriental carpet, the black leather and velvet plush of the instrument cases—all of it suddenly overwhelmed Lawrence with its gorgeousness. The music now, like a kind of sustained excitement in counterpoint, seemed an expression of, or an answer to, the beauty all around it. Juliana caught Lawrence's eye and smiled in greeting.

When the movement ended, there was an explosion of appreciation, comment, and laughter. The musicians themselves, wiry men of middle age, were perhaps heartiest in response, clapping one another on the back and shaking hands. Two of the male musicians left their chairs and were replaced by a man and a young woman. They located their entrances in the score, tuned briefly, then sat up alert, bows poised to play. The music, charged with new energy, resumed.

Juliana sidestepped her way gingerly around to Lawrence and squeezed his hand. They listened to the movement in silence, then clapped loudly with the others.

"It's so unreal to see you here," Juliana said to him. "Welcome to bedlam." She gestured past the musicians, to the hallway, traversed busily at the moment by elderly ladies bearing plates laden with blintzes and gefilte fish, to the sitting rooms beyond, where small children raced about the obstacle course of furniture and seated relatives.

"It is unreal," Lawrence said. "But it's wonderful."

"Anna Lisa!" one of the players called out. "It is time for Anna Lisa!" Elsewhere about the room and from the corridor behind, the cry for Anna Lisa was taken up.

"I'll find her," Juliana said, and left Lawrence gripping the neck of her cello.

A moment later, Juliana emerged from the kitchen, holding the hand of a young girl of about ten. She, like Juliana, was dressed in a white blouse and long skirt, and like Juliana, she was angular, dark, and beautiful. She held a violin and bow in one hand, and as she entered the circle of players, she broke into a smile.

"We can't play the Mozart without Anna Lisa!" one of the players said.

As the players tuned and the listeners chatted, Juliana helped arrange the girl's music.

"Who is that little beauty?" Lawrence asked Juliana. "Your sister?"

"One of my sisters. Anna Lisa, the real talent of the house—"

"Are the others here?"

"Yes. Somewhere. You can't miss the Franck beak." Juliana tapped her lovely nose. "Gretchen and Grace Marie."

"Do they all play?"

"Everybody plays," said Juliana.

The music resumed. The little girl was extraordinary, Lawrence thought. He could not distinguish the excellence of her playing from that of the adults around her, but it was the quality of close attention, her surrender to what surely must have seemed to her an ancient, classical task that moved Lawrence to the brink of tears. That such a fresh and delicate little girl could give herself so completely to a convention so exacting seemed amazing to Lawrence.

Surrender. That was it. The Franck girls have the capacity—the gift—of surrendering themselves.

By the time Anna Lisa's quartet had ended, Lawrence was beginning to feel leg-weary, and he welcomed Rachel Franck's invitation to sample the buffet. In the breakfast room beyond, tables covered with white linen joined together and supported what was to Lawrence an overwhelming display of food: fruit and nuts in aspic, salmon mousse, thin rolls of smoked salmon, sardines, cheeses, blintzes, glazed fruits, pickles, gefilte fish, dumplings, schnitzel, melon balls in whipped cream, bagels, rye and pumpernickel loaves.

Lawrence filled a china plate and was moving back toward the entrance hall and, he hoped, a chair, when Julius Franck crossed to him, smiling broadly.

"Mr. Lawrence! You honor us."

"The honor is mine. What wonderful music. And what wonderful food."

Julius Franck surveyed Lawrence's plate. "You have barely started, Mr. Lawrence. Let me get you a glass of wine. Gretchen! Gretchen, darling, get Mr. Lawrence a glass of wine, will you?"

Gretchen, perhaps fourteen, also dark, the familiar Franck beauty emergent in her slightly horsey face, retreated into the kitchen.

Deciding the sitting rooms were full to overflowing, Lawrence seated himself on the stairs at the rear of the entrance hall. Gretchen Franck appeared, carrying a glass of pink wine, and looked vacantly into the sitting rooms.

"Here I am," called Lawrence. "I think I'm your customer."

The girl turned to him and brightened. It was Juliana's smile. She handed him the glass.

"Are you Mr. Lawrence, Juliana's teacher?"

"I'm not her teacher. I'm her guidance counselor."

"That's what I meant." Gretchen Franck looked as if she meant to stay. "Do you know Paul?"

"Paul Berrisford? Yes. I'm his guidance counselor, too."

"Do you see him very often?"

"Pretty often. Most days actually. Why?"

"I was just wondering. He used to go out with Juliana. He used to come over a lot."

"Maybe he will again."

Gretchen Franck looked away. "I don't think so."

Lawrence was about to ask her about her music and her schoolwork, when she turned back to him. "Did you give Paul and Juliana that picture?"

"I did give them a picture. A copy of one I have in my office. They both admired it, so I gave it to them."

"Juliana had the picture in her room, then it was gone, now it's back."

"Mm," said Lawrence. "What do you think is going on? Do you think she's deciding if she likes it?"

"Oh, she likes it—"

"Gretchen!" Yet another near-Juliana rushed into the entrance hall. "Gretchen—oh, I'm sorry. I'm interrupting." Grace Marie, an even gradation in development between Gretchen and Juliana, approached Lawrence and offered him her hand. "You're Mr. Lawrence, aren't you? I've seen you at school. I'm Grace Marie, Juliana's sister."

"And Gretchen's sister," said Gretchen.

"Yes," said Grace Marie with pretended archness. Squarer of face than Juliana, Gretchen wore her thick black hair above her shoulders. Her eyes were large and very green. *Another beauty,* Lawrence told himself, *but a variation.*

"Oh—Gretchen, we're supposed to play. They want us for the new Hindemith things."

"Oh, I love those," said Gretchen, rising. "Come listen when you're done, Mr. Lawrence. They're really beautiful."

Lawrence raised his glass in valediction, then listened to the delicate Hindemith miniatures from his solitary place on the stairs. *What a strange, sweet wine this is,* Lawrence thought, *yet nearly undrinkable, except by imagining it as some beverage other than wine.*

Still, it was an appropriate complement to the sweet, heavy meal he had just eaten on the stairs, and now, as he swallowed the last of it, he found it agreeably warming. Lawrence surveyed the activity in the rooms on either side of the entrance hall. *This,* he decided, *is a complete world.*

Someone was calling Juliana to the music room. A moment later, she appeared under the archway to the sitting rooms, a hand delicately upon the shoulder of a very old woman. "Are you calling me?" she sang out across the hallway.

"We must have Juliana!" came the voice again. "It is adagio time. Come in here, mistress of the adagio."

Juliana smiled beautifully, said something into the ear of the ancient relative, and crossed to the music room. Lawrence followed.

A quartet had formed in the center of the room, and a fifth man was distributing music to the newly assembled players. "Barber this evening? Elgar? Walton?"

"Oh, let's play them all," Juliana said. "We'll reduce the household to tears."

"Grateful tears," said the gentleman distributing the scores.

Finally in agreement, they were poised to play. As the room quieted, Lawrence thought he observed—was sure of it, in fact—that the attention of the other men in the room, everyone's attention, was as intensely fixed on Juliana as his own was. *Every honest man is in love with every thoroughly beautiful woman.*

Lawrence let himself take in the full force of her image: above her black dance slippers, her swathed knees bowed apart to accommodate the cello, her slender fingers arched and sure on the fingerboard, the bow barely held in her right hand. Her hair fell forward from the red velvet band, closely wreathing her face. Juliana, now lost in the score, surrendered to it, like her sister. The piece, unfamiliar to him, was very simple and very sweet.

Lawrence became aware of the room as a single composition. Though the players and some of the listeners were in motion, they also presented something of a tableau. Juliana, at its center, was its star. Nothing in the room suggested the era, even the century. The polished wood, the reds of the carpet and the damask, the wine through the facets of the glasses—this was a careful, loving recreation. For all Lawrence knew, it might have been the Francks' Vienna.

In any event, it pointed to Europe, it pointed back. Juliana, Lawrence realized, was a living expression of what these close and gentle people valued, not a prodigy of their ambition, not someone they hoped to thrust outward onto the world, but an expression of remembered beauty.

In this, he thought, how unlike Paul she was. Whereas Paul was so manifestly a Berrisford maverick, as disconnected from the world of his parents as he could make himself, Juliana belonged in this sweet, rich room.

CHAPTER *Nine*

Lawrence saw Paul and Juliana only in passing during the week that followed. It occurred to him that it was the first week since he had made their acquaintance in the fall that he had not had a sustained visit from either of them. Both looked especially well, he thought, and on Friday, when Lawrence noticed Juliana leaving the cafeteria as he was going in, he thought her color had returned, along with some other vibrant quality he could not identify. Smiling in recognition, she seemed somehow to be emanating light. *That girl has not lost the power to stir me,* Lawrence said to himself

It was to be a long Memorial Day weekend. Lawrence did not especially look forward to the added day's quiet. The unstructured summer months lay only two weeks ahead. He did not need Memorial Day. Memorial Day, like Labor Day and the more recently designated Presidents' Day, evoked no special anticipation or memory in him. They were days when mail was not delivered, and when the dry cleaners were likely closed.

He had not gotten around to calling Alix Devereaux, and he had no plans or obligations whatever for the long weekend.

Lawrence felt a sudden, unbidden pang of loneliness. The unassignable feeling of irritation he had felt on rising that Friday morning intensified to something like anxiety as the school afternoon wore on. Lawrence wondered, uncomfortably, if he might be drinking too much coffee.

That afternoon, leaving school a half hour early, he set out at a brisk pace on foot in the direction of the lake. Immediately, he felt better. He made his way past the Franck house without so much as an exploratory glance. He traveled a serrated mile and a half to the Berrisfords', a rambling old suburban villa of cinnamon-colored stucco, forbidding-looking even in the soft, late afternoon light. So far as Lawrence could tell, the house was unoccupied.

By six, Lawrence had doubled back to the city center, past the Orrington Hotel—where he considered calling, but did not call, Alix—and past the handsome facade of apartments leased for life to the elderly well-to-do. A rush of lake breeze reinvigorated him, and he swung southward down Sheridan Road, alert to the streaming traffic, and glad of the lake's vastness at his side.

Then, midway between Evanston center and the Chicago city line, Lawrence stopped, peered out over the lake's humped horizon, and reversed direction. *I should be hungry,* Lawrence thought, *but I am not.* He committed himself to a long walk, a walk perhaps of record duration.

Lawrence remembered an article he was considering writing. A month earlier, he had entered these words in the cryptic, erratic journal he kept: *article idea—"Theology, Not Psychology."* It had been a long time—years—since he had written anything for publication. He liked to think of himself, and to think of his colleagues regarding him, when and if they did, as "having written a few articles."

"Theology, Not Psychology." Lawrence walked on, almost unseeing, trying to recapture the twinge of excitement, of connection, he had felt when he made the entry in his journal. Then teasingly, fleetingly, it came back to him. Psychology, despite whole mass-market magazines given over to its promise, does not help. Psychology cannot help. Psychology— "counseling," "therapy," "treatment," "analysis," "encounters," "support"—can proceed only so long as psychologists and their "clients" do not ask the main question: "What is this for? How am I supposed to live?"

Psychology, Lawrence reflected, striding evenly over the damp concrete, assumes a personality's proper alignment with its surroundings. Psychologists proceed as if proper alignment were a knowable, positive, comfortable condition.

Psychology cannot deliver anything. Lawrence felt he knew this much. He was a psychologist, a guidance counselor. Lawrence thought: *What we psychologists try for is a slightly smoother version of what everybody else tries for in the face of trou-*

ble or tension or fear; we try to calm things down. If we can't calm things down, we assist in removing the troubled party from the scene. If we can't do that, we tend to remove ourselves from the scene. We cure nobody, Lawrence said to himself. We don't know how. Psychology doesn't know how.

He proceeded, northward now, back toward the university. The rhythm of his walking, the rumble from the highway, the gusting of the soft lake air—all cohered agreeably. I will walk, Lawrence allowed, as far as the Berrisfords' beach house in Wilmette, if I can find it. Lawrence convinced himself that the beach house was no more than a northern terminus, a landmark. He would not snoop. He did not care to see Paul and Juliana even in the unlikely event that they were there.

The sun receded behind the rooftops of the residences to his left. The facades grew dark in the smoky light. Lawrence walked on, swallowing back wave upon wave of a feeling he could not name.

Night had fallen when Lawrence passed beyond the Evanston line. Suddenly he was full of doubt. In memory, the lane leading to the Berrisford beach house appeared almost immediately after crossing the city line. But that had been in Alix's car. Now, on foot, in this dusky light, Lawrence was not sure. He passed two lanes, or driveways, which did not feel at all familiar. I have gone too far, Lawrence thought; I have gone almost a mile. Then he saw it, exactly as he had remembered.

Lawrence turned off the highway to his right.

With every step, it seemed, he grew more aware of the water. Ahead, beyond the tree line, he could hear the lake's great rush and rumble. As the road surface changed from asphalt to earth, Lawrence could feel the air become cooler, almost chilly. He proceeded along the path in darkness.

From the steep ridge beyond the cul-de-sac, Lawrence could see the black horizon arch enormously, ominously. Tiny pink and green lights from buoys and boats pierced the hazy darkness like stars. Lawrence let the firm wind from the lake meet his face. *An utterly inhospitable body of water,* Lawrence reflected. Even now, even in soft May, it was dark and harsh and menacing: somehow massively dead.

Lawrence turned toward the beach house. The window in the side door revealed an uneven, flickering light inside. Lawrence was not surprised. As he drew closer to the house, the darkness deepened to the point that Lawrence could not see his feet.

What am I doing? he asked himself, almost aloud. *What am I doing?* Within a yard of the step leading to the side door, Lawrence stopped. *I don't want to knock,* he thought. *I don't even want to talk to them. It might well be somebody else inside; it was a shared property.*

Lawrence moved his feet carefully over the high weeds lining the path. He made his way uncomfortably to the back wall of the building, where it met the limestone face rising steeply behind it. From the rear of the house, Lawrence could see the light flickering over the rounded top of a gas or water tank.

Between the back wall and the limestone ridge, there was an overgrown corridor of three or four feet. Lawrence edged himself around the back of the building. Inching along until he reached the metal tank, Lawrence put his ear to the wall of the building but heard nothing.

A line of screened windows ran about a foot above Lawrence's head. By stepping up onto the concrete base supporting the tank and then onto an outcropping of limestone from the ledge behind him, Lawrence found that, by inclining his weight forward onto the sill below the screen, he could look inside.

At first he saw nothing, then a line of light at the floor level. Back bedrooms, Lawrence guessed. By sliding his feet along the ledge and his hands along the sills, Lawrence passed from window to window. The interior door to the adjacent room had been left open, and through its frame Lawrence could see into the sitting room he had visited several weeks before.

Irregular shafts of light from an unseen fire projected shadows, and occasionally great voids of blackness, on the forms within. By edging to the next window, Lawrence could make out the figures of Paul and Juliana. Lawrence felt a strange, melting wave of weakness, a sensation that made him aware of the actual strain on his arms from supporting himself against the wall. He considered dropping to ground level, making his way quietly back to the drive, to the highway, and home. But he did not.

The screening was scarred and pitted in places, and the window glass was filmy with the winter's grime, but when the lights flared, Lawrence could see Paul and Juliana with a special clarity. Paul's naked back—peach and orange-colored in the firelight—was visible above a low haphazard wall of cushions and firewood. He appeared to be kneeling, directly facing Juliana, whose long black hair fell to her bare shoulders. The rest of Juliana was blocked from view by Paul's torso.

Juliana's face, downcast and abstracted, appeared deeply thoughtful to Lawrence. She was clearly not speaking. Nor, Lawrence surmised, was Paul, although Lawrence could see only the back of his tousled head. There was something ritualistic, votive, about their kneeling postures.

The light wavered darkly, and Paul looked to the right, in the direction of the fire. A second later, he picked up a log from the pile at hand and moved out of view. When the light suddenly flared up again, Lawrence could see Juliana more clearly. Still distracted, she stared in the direction of the fire. She, too, was naked, and her hair fell down along the outer curve of each breast, creating, in the firelight, the impression of an Indian squaw.

Lawrence felt another, stronger wave of weakness. She was very beautiful. From the outset, he had noted Juliana's slenderness and almost gothic angularity. But this fullness, this creamy ripeness, he had never imagined, never tried to imagine. *There is this, too,* Lawrence realized. *This, too, is what Paul knows.* Lawrence let himself look at Juliana. *She is perfect.*

Paul, still in a crouch, moved back to face Juliana. Again, some ritual seemed to resume. Lawrence was aware of a blast of lake wind sweeping over the rooftop above his head. The noise somehow intensified the silence of the tableau before him. Paul placed his hands gently upon Juliana's shoulders, and she looked into his eyes.

For what seemed to Lawrence a long time, they did not move. When the throbbing in his wrists and arms became unbearable, Lawrence pushed himself painfully back from the sill and dropped to the ground. Knees, wrists, and elbows ached, and Lawrence felt rigidly cold as he stood in the dark corridor behind the house.

He stepped gingerly back to the cul-de-sac and turned once more to look at the beach house and the lake. The vast arc of dark water seemed, if anything, even more overpowering. Through the small panes of glass in the beach house door, Lawrence could see the flicker of reflected firelight, blues now alternating with peach and pink. Lawrence turned and strode off down the dark, rustling lane.

It was past midnight when he crossed the city line back into Evanston. His legs felt heavy and spent beneath him, a sensation by no means unfamiliar to him from numerous, nocturnal walks. Rarely, however, had he reached this particular point of leg-weariness with so many miles between him and the carriage house.

Despite his fatigue, Lawrence felt agitated and alert. The image of Juliana, all cream and repose in the firelight, presented itself repeatedly before his mind's eye. *That such a girl could even exist,* he said to himself. Although vaguely aroused since leaving the beach house, he had not felt any momentum toward lovemaking on Paul and Juliana's part, but rather a stillness, almost worshipful.

Lawrence found himself both surprised and not surprised by their nakedness: the intimacy they had obviously achieved. They had always been affectionate with each other in his company. But nothing in the impulsive clasp of arm around shoulder, the squeeze of a hand, or the stroking of Juliana's cheek had suggested to Lawrence any barely contained sexual energy by either of them. *But what do I know,* Lawrence thought. As he reached Sheridan Road, Lawrence recalled Paul's surprising answer to his inquiry about whether he had considered marrying Juliana: "We are married . . . If there's a God, then we're married forever before Him. We've seen to that."

"Ritual," Lawrence said out loud. In night silence, he passed the comfortable brick houses lining the avenues approaching the university. The fan windows over the entrances revealed, now and again, a soft light within. Otherwise, the streets were agreeably desolate, the warm gusts that passed through the elms overhead carrying none of the harsh bite of wind at the lakefront.

The *ritual,* Lawrence thought; *also the stillness, and the sadness.* Lawrence felt as if he were working on an equation too elusive and too complex. Paul and Juliana had conveyed nothing of a teenage couple on a furtive, possibly erotic, rendezvous. Something else was at work.

Lawrence suddenly entertained an image of the great dark sweep of lake against the horizon—then an image of another body of dark water: the Irish Sea, Evelyn Waugh, and the story of the comically failed suicide Lawrence had told Paul and Juliana about earlier at the beach house. That had been funny, Lawrence recalled. Paul and Juliana had been especially attentive.

Lawrence stopped short on the pavement. *Oh, my Lord Jesus Christ.* Quickening his pace to a jog, which sent searing pains along the line where thigh met torso, Lawrence hurried back toward Wilmette and the beach house. Then, a block later, he stopped, wheeled again, and headed toward his own house, blind now to the features of the darkened city. *I'll get there faster by car,* Lawrence told himself. *Oh, my Lord Jesus Christ.*

Lawrence arrived at the back stairs to the carriage house leg-heavy and befuddled, but alive with nervous energy. He climbed the steps, moved through his darkened kitchen, and, without turning on the bedroom light, opened the top drawer of his desk. He foraged clumsily through the loose change, pens, nails, screws, and odd bits of hardware before his fingers closed on the outsized head of the ignition key to the Renault.

Lawrence switched on the lights of the carriage house garage. There, in the bright yellow light, stood the Renault. Even in the anonymous surroundings of the old garage, the lines of the car struck Lawrence as arresting, incongruous. He walked around the car, looking critically at the tires: low but drivable. *It's been months,* thought Lawrence, moving to the light panel.

Upstairs, the phone rang jarringly. Lawrence bounded up the stairs on aching legs.

"Is this . . . um . . . Mr. Lawrence from Evanston High School?"

"Yes, it is."

"Oh, God. Mr. Lawrence, this is Sally Berrisford, Paul Berrisford's sister. I'm really sorry to be calling in the middle of the night, but I have a problem, and I need help."

"Yes, it's all right. What's up?"

"I'm supposed to be staying with my brother—watching him actually—while my parents are away, and he's gone. He was working upstairs after supper, and I thought he was still there, but he's gone."

"I'm sure he'll be all right," said Lawrence.

"Normally, I'm sure he would be, too. But my parents have been really worried about him lately. They were afraid he'd run away for a while. I know he's with his girl somewhere, but I can't imagine where. All the cars are here. His bike is here. I can't think where to look."

"Have you told anyone?" Lawrence asked.

"I didn't want to call my parents until I was sure he's really gone. But maybe I should anyway. I don't think there's any reason to call the police, do you? And I just can't call the girl's parents. But maybe I should do that, too. What do you think? Oh, I'm not making any sense, am I?"

"Of course you are. It's probably nothing. Paul tends to do whatever comes into his head. Why don't you stay there and wait for him, and I'll take a look around the city—I know some of his haunts. If he doesn't turn up by morning, then you'd better get in touch with your parents."

"But do you think I should call the girl's house? I mean, I'd hate it if I were her parents."

"Let me think about that. I know the Francks."

"Fine. I'd just as soon not have to rouse them in the middle of the night."

"Okay then, why don't you just keep an eye out for him there? Let me see what I can find out. But if Paul's not back by morning, I really think you should call your parents."

"I think you're right. I wouldn't be in such a panic if Paul hadn't been behaving so strangely lately . . . I don't think he'd mind that I called you. He really likes you. He's really a great person most of the time, but he could do anything. He's been strange since I've been home. Well, okay, I'll look out for him. Thanks again, Mr. Lawrence. This is above and beyond—oh."

"What is it?"

"We have a beach house," she said. "We have a beach house in Wilmette we share with my uncle's family. I wonder if he could've gone there for the night. I wonder if he ever does that."

"Where is it?" Lawrence said flatly. Sally Berrisford gave him the directions.

"I may check there, too," said Lawrence.

"Oh, you're terrific. Thank you."

The Renault's engine sounded to Lawrence as if it might shake itself apart. Gradually, as he held the accelerator pedal down, the pumping of the cylinders began to approximate the rumbling sequence of an internal combustion engine. Typically, after a bad start like this one, Lawrence recalled, the Renault seemed to find its rhythm after a few blocks in motion.

Lawrence could not help smiling as the car putted and popped along the drive past the big house. He thought about his rusted Connecticut license plates, expired for nearly twenty years. *What are you doing, Lawrence?* He was careful to observe all lights and signs on the way to Wilmette.

As he turned onto the lane to the beach house, Lawrence was sharply aware of the Renault's imperfectly muffled engine. *They'll hear me coming a mile away and bolt,* he thought.

The beach house was dark when Lawrence shut off the Renault's engine in the cul-de-sac. *Perhaps they've gone,* he thought, realizing how awkward it would be to turn up unexpectedly. He peered into the sitting room through the side-door window. Some embers were still burning in the fireplace. Otherwise, the room looked vacant. Lawrence hesitated, then knocked crisply. There was silence. He knocked again.

"Hello," he called out. "Hello."

Lawrence waited on the chilly stoop. To his left, the sky was lightening over the lake. He pounded hard on the glass this time. "Paul, Juliana. Hello?"

Lawrence turned the handle and opened the door. He sang out another hello. In the sitting room, he switched on a table lamp. The room had been hastily tidied, the firewood stacked to one side of the hearth, the cushions stacked on the other. An Indian blanket was folded and draped over the back of a wicker sofa.

"Paul? Juliana?"

Lawrence was about to explore the back corridor and sleeping rooms when he spotted the note on the mantelpiece. A sheet of ruled notebook paper had been folded over twice and pressed against the mantel stone by a glass ashtray. Lawrence removed the note and opened it. The script was elegantly careful: Juliana's.

To our families and our friends,

As you have found out by now, we are together. We are not being defiant together, nor are we being reckless or headstrong together. We are just together, and although we are worried about you and your disappointment in us, we are very happy.

We love each other. We wish you could know how much. Nothing matters to us more than this. We are sure it is what we were born for. If you don't understand this, or believe it, please try to forgive it—and to think as well of us as you can.

We have no regrets at all. We have been and are right now unimaginably happy.

Our love spills over to you—forever.

Oh, my Lord Jesus Christ. Lawrence placed the note back on the mantel, covered it with the ashtray, and rushed outside. In the grainy gray-green light, he could see only dark rocks and gray patches of sand at the bottom of the nearly vertical wooden steps. Holding the damp handrails securely, Lawrence began negotiating the steps down to the water.

Below, on the beach, the dark waves broke and ran to within a few yards of the steps. Directly in front of him, just beyond the line where the water had smoothed and darkened the sand, Lawrence spotted two neatly folded mounds of clothes. Crouching to inspect them, he saw that they had been arranged with some care to cover Paul and Juliana's shoes, the toes of which pointed out into the leaden surf. Lawrence stood up to ease his aching knees.

"Paul! Juliana!"

He considered climbing back up the stairs, finding a phone, calling the Coast Guard, the Francks, Sally Berrisford.

Lawrence shouted their names repeatedly.

The low lines of waves revealed nothing. Lawrence retreated to the steps and sat down. He felt too tired and dull-witted to think through this emergency. He felt close to tears—tears of exhaustion.

"Paul!" Lawrence cried, this time gasping. "Juliana!"

Lawrence's gaze was fixed directly ahead, perhaps twenty yards out into the water, and that's where Paul's head and shoulders first emerged. Lawrence stood. Paul turned on his side and stroked once in the direction of shore. When the momentum of this surge was entirely spent, he bobbed uncertainly for a moment and stroked again. Not more than two yards from where the waves broke on the beach, Paul stood, stumbled to his knees, and stood again.

"Paul!"

Paul grunted something incoherent, then turned his back to Lawrence. With more force, he hollered, "There, Jewel, you're *there*, Jewel."

And there, at the same point in the featureless surf where Lawrence had first spotted Paul, Juliana's dark, matted head rose out of the void.

Lawrence moved to the water's edge. "Can I help?" he shouted.

There was no answer. Lawrence stooped to feel the water as a foamy sheet surrounded his shoes. It was shockingly cold on his skin.

Paul turned and stepped heavily and stiff-legged to the shore. He reached down for Juliana's linen jacket and long skirt, then splashed back into the shallow surf to guide her in and to cover her.

Lawrence could hear Juliana now: a repetitive, shuddering moan, a bleating like some kind of animal.

"Are you all right?" Lawrence asked, feeling ineffectual.

Paul swaddled Juliana with her clothing and ran a hand rapidly over her back.

Paul mumbled something thickly, pointing a finger up the wooden steps. Then, more clearly: "Run some water. Some hot water in the tub, please."

"Right," Lawrence responded, glad of an assigned, manageable task. He made his way on rubbery legs up the steps to the beach house, located a bathroom, stabilized the water at its hottest, and began filling the tub. Back outside, he could see Paul guiding Juliana slowly toward the base of the steps. Lawrence hurried back down to help her, still shuddering, up the stairway.

"Are you all right?" Lawrence asked again.

"All right," said Paul. "Cold."

"Anybody stung by a jellyfish?"

"Cold," said Paul.

As they proceeded one step at a time up to the beach house, the sky behind them grew brilliant, replete with striated pinks and pale greens. Inside the house, Paul and Juliana moved to the bath, and Lawrence descended the steps once more to retrieve the rest of their clothes and their shoes. The sky was now shot through with shafts of rose, radiant yellows, and lavender. Lawrence felt a swelling of gratitude and happiness.

It was not the world everyone imagines.

Lawrence collapsed onto the wicker sofa and waited for Paul and Juliana to emerge. Sleep would have been welcome, but it did not come. The room brightened, and he could hear fragments of Paul and Juliana's talk, even laughter.

Paul, impressively restored in white linen trousers and a heavily cabled sweater, entered the room. He carried a half-filled pillowcase over his shoulder.

"How're you doing?" he greeted Lawrence and smiled.

"Pretty well, thanks, and you?"

Paul laughed. "Better than an hour ago. That"—Paul gestured toward the lake—"is not for us. That's like putting your whole body into a giant, freezing-cold vise. I'll tell you, that's death out there."

"And that's not what you want."

"No, that's definitely not what we want."

Paul looked behind him toward the back hallway and lowered his voice. "Mr. Lawrence, I want to—it feels really strange even talking about this, and we're going to fly out of here in a minute—but I have to tell you one thing. When we were out there in the water, and I was starting to feel numb, and Juliana wasn't talking anymore, an amazing thing happened. For a few seconds, I couldn't see Jewel at all, then she came up just behind me. She couldn't talk. I said to myself, 'You're *killing* this girl, you're killing her.' It was like a terrific electric shock that went on and on. And I was sure we couldn't get back. I was trying to say 'back' and I couldn't do it. I couldn't make the *b* sound.

"When I reached for Juliana, I think I scared her. She was trying so hard to stay up, to keep moving. And then I heard you. You sounded so close. I thought we were in the middle of the lake, but the whole way back you sounded about three feet away. It was good to hear you, Mr. Lawrence."

"But," Paul continued, opening the doors to the cupboards lining the wall, "we've got to make some plans fast." Paul sorted through a stack of folded sweaters and flannel shirts, stuffing some of them into the pillowcase.

"Who knows we're here?" he asked Lawrence.

"I do," Lawrence said. "And your sister Sally suspects it."

"You talked to Sally?"

"Mm."

"What did she say?"

"She said you were missing."

"Did she call my folks or my uncle?"

"I don't think so. She was going to wait until morning."

"Okay," said Paul, seemingly oblivious to Lawrence. "Okay."

"What's okay?"

"Mr. Lawrence," Paul said, "how did you get here?"

"I drove."

"Drove what, Miss Devereaux's car?"

"No, my own."

Paul brightened. "You did? You mean the Dauphine?"

"Yes," said Lawrence. "At great personal risk."

Juliana emerged from the back hall. Strings of her hair, still glistening wet, fell forward over her shoulders. She had put on a much-laundered man's flannel shirt and a pair of khaki trousers, cinched into her waist with a leather belt. She looked wonderful, Lawrence thought.

"I won't even ask what you think of all this," Juliana said.

"Well, then I won't tell you."

"Thank goodness. Paul, whose things are these? Won't they be missed?"

"They're nobody's. They've always been here."

Paul disappeared into the back hall, returning with their wet clothes over his arm. "I'll be right back."

"Where are you going?" Juliana asked.

"Down to the beach."

"For a swim?" said Lawrence.

"Too cold," said Paul, on his way out.

Juliana left the room and came back in a moment, toting another pillowcase, presumably stuffed with clothing. She dragged both sacks along the floor to the side door.

"Going somewhere?" Lawrence said.

"I think we'd better," said Juliana.

Lawrence rose from the sofa and peered out the window

over the ledge to the beach. Below, Paul was bent over the wet clothing, carefully arranging it in two mounds, just beyond the reach of the waves.

"Do you feel all right now?" Lawrence asked Juliana.

"I feel wonderful," said Juliana. "Tired, but completely wonderful. It feels like everything is about to start."

Lawrence considered her comment in silence. He felt a nagging obligation to offer some guidance, even a stern warning of some kind, but could not determine clearly what it should be.

Paul entered the sitting room from the side door. He regarded the two pillowcases at his feet.

"Mr. Lawrence," he said. "We need your help. I know I can't ask you to lie or to cover up for us, but I'd sure appreciate it if you didn't have to report all this on your own. Maybe you have to—I don't know what's legal. But anyway, I think we have a fair chance to make it, if we can just get a head start."

"Make what? Exactly where are you off to?"

"I don't think I should tell you. Sorry. But it'll be easier for you that way. Oh, hey—one more thing. This is a real favor, and you don't have to do it."

"What is it?"

"Could you maybe straighten things up here a little after we go? Just sort of put things back where they belong? You know," he said, "even things like this fire. You could spread out the coals, and if you could wait a bit until they're absolutely cold, then there'll be no . . . no danger."

"So you want me to stay here until the fire is cold?" Lawrence could not help smiling through his fatigue.

"If you could."

"I think I'm up to a job like that," said Lawrence. "On one condition. That, wherever it is you're going, you promise to be careful."

"Promise," said Paul.

Juliana crossed to the sofa and hugged Lawrence until her arms began to tremble.

"You've been wonderful," she said.

Lawrence couldn't speak. He saluted them, stupidly, he thought, as they went out the door. Lawrence slid down into a reclining position on the sofa.

It could have been a minute later or twenty minutes—he had dropped off to sleep—when Lawrence heard the noisy rumble of a car. He rose without thinking, his mind racing with explanations. Even before he reached the side-door window, however, Lawrence recognized the intrusive rumble as the engine of the Renault. As he peered out after it, the car lurched forward, then began sputtering down the lane, only the two pillowcases visible through the tiny oval of the car's rear window.

Lawrence smiled, then laughed out loud.

Feeling light-headed, his stomach slightly cramped rather than hungry, Lawrence moved to the back rooms of the beach house, starting with the large, old-fashioned bath, and began straightening up. He swabbed the tub dry with a faded beach towel and draped it over a rack to dry—then reconsidered, wadded it into a ball, and wedged it into a corner of a closet shelf. The sleeping and changing rooms, so far as he could tell, had not been disturbed.

Back in the sitting room, Lawrence tamped the last coals down to ash and replaced the hearth screen. He surveyed the room in the blinding morning light. Some sand and damp grit had been tracked between the straw mat by the door and the carpet. That would have to do, Lawrence decided. Bending once, slowly, at the waist and smiling again, he mentally pictured his long walk home to the carriage house.

When he crossed onto the highway from the private lane, Lawrence began to feel better, somehow less guilty. To anyone driving by—police, parent, Sally Berrisford—he would simply be a pedestrian, in no way remarkable.

And the farther he proceeded across the city line into Evanston, the more secure and anonymous he felt.

Then he remembered the note on the mantel. "Idiot," he said aloud. Lawrence stopped to consider returning to the beach house. *No,* he determined, the conviction gaining strength as he walked on. *It's their note, and it expresses their* feelings and wishes . . . And if he were to confiscate the note—did they intend it to stay on the mantel?—wouldn't he have to confiscate their clothes on the beach as well? If he did that, there would be a new plan, not necessarily of Paul and Juliana's making. Lawrence imagined descending and reascending the steps down to the beach. *Oh, God, no,* he thought. *What's done is done.*

⁊ଈ

It was just past noon and a hot, clear day when Lawrence turned down the drive to the carriage house. For blocks, for miles, he had been unaware of any distinction between his thinking and his walking. He felt reduced to his calves and thighs, knees and pelvis.

Lawrence was giddy with triumph as he unlocked his kitchen door and entered his rooms. All was cool and dark inside, the sitting room windows radiant in contrast. Although past hunger, Lawrence drank a tall glass of orange juice and ate a sandwich thick with ham, cheese, mustard, and sprouts.

His apartment looked wonderful—all quiet and order. Lawrence drew down his bedroom shade, unplugged the phone from its jack, undressed, and got into bed.

For a time before sleep came to him, thought broke apart into undirected, dream-like images. Paul's head appeared out of the gray water. All three of them were warming by the fire. It was the Christmas fire from his own hearth . . . Juliana, alone and naked and slightly downcast before the fire . . . The rear of the mustard-colored Renault sputtering into the lane, the two pillowcases, Paul and Juliana disappearing down the sparkling green lane.

Lawrence slept the rest of the day and far into the next.

CHAPTER *Ten*

$\mathbb{F}$or weeks, Lawrence found himself periodically on edge, wondering why no one seemed more interested in finding out what he knew about Paul and Juliana's disappearance. He had no doubt been telephoned frantically a day or two after their disappearance was discovered, but he had not been reachable, and the callers, probably out of necessity, turned elsewhere.

He had carefully rehearsed himself to respond truthfully, but not expansively, to what he believed would be the hardest, and perhaps even incriminating, questions. But, as it happened, he was asked very little.

Prominent pieces appeared in the Chicago papers: "North Shore Teens Feared Drowned in Suicide Pact, School Sweethearts Disappear from Wilmette Beach." To Lawrence, the entire high school complex seemed wounded and subdued throughout exams and graduation.

Student rumors, some of them hysterical, ran rampant for a day or two, then were refuted, only to be supplanted by others. A monograph was distributed to the faculty and the guidance staff about the warning signs of teenage suicide.

A midsummer edition of *Chicago Magazine* ran a feature

on the Berrisfords and the Francks—"When Children Love Too Much: A Family Tragedy in Evanston"—but it was clear to Lawrence that neither family had cooperated fully with the reporter. The story thus fell back on the more sensational details culled from the police report and on the classically tragic structure of the incident. There were photographs of the Franck and Berrisford houses and of the beach house, of Paul and Juliana from the school yearbook, and of the high school buildings. Lawrence marveled at the journalist's inability to touch, much less comprehend, what had actually occurred.

Within a day or two of the first newspaper accounts, Lawrence had written short notes of concern and sympathy to the Francks and the Berrisfords. Neither responded, but Rachel Franck made an appointment to see him in his office on the final day of post-semester staff meetings.

"I don't want to trouble you with our heartache," she said to Lawrence. "But I did want to ask you, as a professional and as somebody who knows my daughter, whether you"—her voice trembled and broke—"whether you think we . . . our actions drove Juliana away." Rachel Franck wept.

As warmly as he could, Lawrence urged her not to blame herself. He told her that, to him, Juliana had always spoken of her parents with love and good humor. He said he believed that only Juliana's strong feelings for Paul had motivated her, nothing else. Lawrence also urged her to take heart, because it seemed impossible to him that Juliana and Paul were dead.

Of course no bodies were recovered, despite an extensive search over the Memorial Day weekend. At the end of the second day of the search, the Coast Guard told the Francks and the Berrisfords that the majority of those lost at any significant distance from shore were never recovered.

"I'm afraid the only thing we can do now is to consider them lost to us," Rachel Franck had said.

When she left his office, Lawrence sat alone in the declining afternoon light. In the hour that followed, he found himself convinced that he had behaved abominably. Apart from some personal need or individual weakness, what could have convinced him to support two headstrong, lovesick teenagers in a flight from their families? What possible good could compensate for the deep grief these parents were feeling now? *I am a knowing party to this deception*, Lawrence told himself, *and I am not an adolescent in love. Right now and with each passing minute, I am perpetrating a cruelty.* Then, just for a moment, it was clear to him: *I have no right to this particular power.*

Lawrence reached for the telephone, but did not pick up the receiver. He would call the police—no, better to talk to the parents first, to tell them exactly what had happened. In all likelihood, within a few days, Paul and Juliana would be found. Back in Evanston, there'd be great confusion and joy-

ful relief. Such feelings might even override any parental incli-
nation to reprove Paul and Juliana further. The two of them
might still—*what?* Lawrence wondered.

Would they be allowed to have one another, entirely and
exclusively? Lawrence recalled how Juliana had looked standing in the early morning light at the beach house door. He
recalled her sitting in his office, tearful that the tantalizing
promise of Arnold's poems and of sun-warmed summer meadows had somehow passed by, been spoiled. "It's true, Mr.
Lawrence, and if they take Paul away from me, then that great
thing will be gone, just like the great things in the poems."
Lawrence looked across his darkened office to the Swabian
lovers. Their faces, luminous against the dark glade behind
them, were frozen in expectation.

To Lawrence, the two detectives who visited him the week
following the couple's disappearance seemed less interested in
learning anything from him than in telling him what, according to the Department's reckoning, had happened.

Juliana, having received her parents' permission to spend
the night with a group of graduating senior girls, had met Paul
late that Friday afternoon, and they had either walked or been
driven to the Wilmette beach house. No vehicle had been
found or observed at the beach house, and police cars and
family cars had covered over any tire marks, although the
Department had checked out what looked like the tread of an

unusual small-gauge car or cycle tire in the cul-de-sac. The two appeared to have spent some time in the house together before writing a note and climbing down to the beach for, as the detective had put it, "their final swim."

"I understand you worked with both these kids," one of the detectives had asked. "What kind of kids were they?"

Lawrence told them that Paul and Juliana were bright, attractive students, both very promising, and that they had fallen deeply in love.

"Why do you think they'd do something like this? To their parents? You think they just couldn't wait?"

"It's hard to see the world the way teenagers see it."

"Were these troubled kids, Mr. Lawrence?"

"I don't think so."

"But they gave it all up."

"Are you sure?" Lawrence asked earnestly.

"If you mean, do we have the bodies? No. They're still missing persons. But if they ran off somewhere, they're without clothes, money, or transportation. And it's been more than a week. Their wallets, their money, identification—everything was left with their clothes on the beach. It doesn't look good."

Almost daily for a week or two after the detectives' call, Lawrence wrestled with one issue. Although almost no one knew he even owned a car, which in any case was neither registered nor insured, it was missing—technically, stolen. If and when it turned up and was traced back to him, there could be trouble. There could be trouble, Lawrence knew, anyway. He decided to report his loss to the Evanston police.

"And you say you don't know the exact day, even the week, when the car was stolen from the garage?" asked the attractive, athletic-looking young woman who processed his report.

"No, I'm afraid not. That must sound strange, but it's not a car I drive. It's just kind of a relic. I go weeks without even looking in the garage."

"Well, Mr. Lawrence, we'll run a check, but I'll be honest with you. We don't find most cars stolen in Evanston. When we do, it's usually a joy rider who picks it up here and leaves it there. We either find them in a day or two after they're reported missing, or we find them stripped and junked somewhere in Chicago. Or we don't find them at all."

"Mm."

"Maybe a collector, maybe someone who needed special parts, stole your car."

"Maybe. It's not a terrific loss. I just thought it was better to report it than to ignore it."

"Well, I hope it turns up."

I hope it never does, Lawrence said to himself.

As the summer wore on, and then the first months of the

new school year, it seemed less and less mysterious to Lawrence that virtually no one had sought him out to talk about Paul and Juliana. Looked at from the standpoint of the Francks or the Berrisfords, he had been no more than a peripheral figure in the drama, a minor factor in their children's school lives, but not a factor in their relationship, or, so far as they knew, in their clandestine meetings and plans outside of school. There was little reason to seek him out.

If they felt he had misadvised the couple, or suspected somehow that he had supported their liaison after it had been prohibited, the parents would understandably want to distance themselves from him. Questioning him directly, even in anger, would be an occasion, possibly, for further grief. And if in the parents' eyes, Lawrence had played only a marginal role, he was certain to be regarded even more marginally by the police and other authorities. At least that would be the case until Paul and Juliana were located.

In that event, Lawrence wondered, what, if anything, might be said on his behalf. His car had, after all, been stolen from him. Lawrence pictured himself under interrogation, attempting to diminish his part in Paul and Juliana's story. His throat constricted at the thought. Paul and Juliana had been— and still were—the very core of his waking experience. There must be some reciprocal feeling on their part, he thought. There must be. *But had he any part in their story?* Had he mattered at all to them?

The rain picked up again, beating heavily, but not disagreeably, on Lawrence's head and face whenever he left the cover of the elms. At a point directly across from the Francks' house, in a reassuring void of streetlight, he stopped to consider the gabled residence. The house was dark—so dark that Lawrence could imagine that it was unoccupied, even abandoned.

He pictured the back of the house: the balustraded roof over the porch where, more than a year before, he had huddled in a similar void of light a few feet below Paul and Juliana's declarations of love. Lawrence told himself that he would gratefully take on all of that night's awkwardness, fear, and cold again in exchange for so much life.

—*So what's next? I keep thinking about it. You can't go away.*

—*How can I ever go away from you? It's not possible. Don't even think about it.*

—*You sound like me.*

—*Good. I like sounding like you. I would like to be you.*

—Then you wouldn't be you, and where would I be?

—You could be me.

—Then we'd be back where we were. Which is heaven. Which is perfect.

A package had been delivered to his home in February, nearly nine months after their disappearance. Beneath his address had been inscribed, in block printing, the words *MERRY CHRISTMAS*.

Inside the padded envelope was a record: a new, unopened recording of Ralph Vaughan Williams's *Oxford Elegy*.

The postage was Canadian, and the badly eroded postal markings on the envelope may have indicated Ontario.

But that was it. No card. No note. No message at all.

Lawrence's head was at once full of half-reaped fields, country churchyards, and other melancholy images from the Arnold poems.

Roam on! The light we sought is shining still.
Dost thou ask proof! Our tree yet crowns the hill,
Our scholar travels yet the loved hillside.

Lawrence walked on, inexplicably happy.